WHERE SHE FELL

Kaitlin Ward

SCHOLASTIC PRESS • NEW YORK

Library of Congress Cataloging-in-Publication Data Available

ISBN 978-1-338-23007-9

10 9 8 7 6 5 4 3 2 1   18 19 20 21 22 23

Printed in the U.S.A.   23

First edition, November 2018

Book design by Maeve Norton

Photography © 2018 by Michael Frost

To Michael, my little geologist

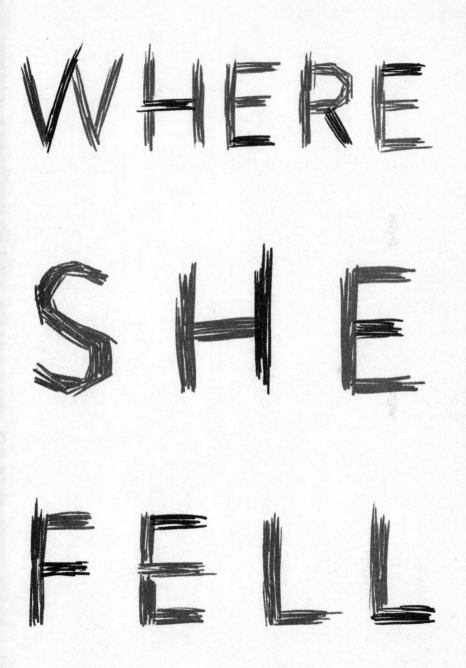

1

Life is just a series of moments that you frame to make yourself look like the hero. That's something my friend Sherri likes to say. *It's not fun if it's not a little bit stupid* is another thing she says.

Sherri is excellent at being both the hero and fun. I am excellent at neither.

It's an unreasonably warm spring day, and my parents consider AC a waste of money, so I'm already sweating at 8:30 in the morning. My backpack lies empty on my bed, looking deflated. I leave it and stand in front of my window fan, gazing out over the driveway like that'll make Sherri and my other best friend, Meg, magically appear, even though it'll be at least another half hour before they do.

Lately, I haven't been that excited when they come over. Meg and I have been best friends since grade school. Sherri joined us at the beginning of ninth. I never expected how this would change things, but here we are.

Today I *am* excited, though. Yesterday, even as it made my

entire body go numb, I texted them both that I wanted us to go cave exploring, and they actually agreed.

I turn back to my bed and my empty bag. If we're going into a cave, I need to fill it with supplies, but I've put it off. Part of me keeps expecting Sherri to text and say she's found something better for us to do today. Something social. Something that'll make me come home feeling like a wrung-out sponge.

After a light knock, my partially open door widens and my younger sister Mara's face pokes through. Mara's fifteen; our birthdays are almost exactly a year apart. She's loud and pretty and extroverted. The sort of person who can take a hundred selfies in a row and look perfect in all of them. Who came out of the womb knowing how to use makeup. People want to hate her, but not as much as they want to befriend her.

"I can't find my mascara," Mara says. "Can I borrow yours? I asked Claire and she said she doesn't want my eye germs."

"Borrow whatever you want." I gesture to my dresser, which has a semi-organized array of jewelry and beauty products sitting atop it. Mara always asks Claire for things before she asks me and I don't know why she bothers. Claire is the oldest, and very protective of her stuff.

"Thanks." Mara starts pawing through the stuff on my dresser. She turns back to me with her fist clenched around a mascara tube and an eye shadow palette. "What are you up to today?"

"Gonna take Sherri and Meg to that cave Claire and I found last weekend."

Mara wrinkles her nose. "How are we related?"

I laugh, because she says it with affection. My sisters and I are very different people, but we get along pretty well anyway. Most of the time. "If one of us is adopted, it's definitely you."

She sticks out her tongue but doesn't contradict me. "Well, don't die out there."

"I'll try not to."

She whisks out the door, and I watch her retreating back. Sometimes I envy Mara. The easy way she interacts with people. How she's always wrapped up in the kind of Teenage Experience that Sherri thinks I should be more interested in, and it's just her nature. School may not come as easily for her as it does for me, but school's going to end someday. Interacting with other people is forever. Which is why I force myself to practice even when it turns my heart into a hummingbird.

With a sigh, I start filling up my backpack. Sherri and Meg are absolutely *not* going to come prepared, so I need to bring plenty—at least when it comes to snacks and lights. I start with a tiny observation journal. I have journals strewn all over the place in here, but I don't like people to see what I've written, so I pack a blank one in case we see something neat. I fold a spare outfit on top of that, in case I get dirty, and a light jacket in case it gets cold. A flashlight, cheap headlamp, and pocket-knife on top of that. The small first-aid kit my mom insists upon goes on top. Several snacks in the front pocket, and a water bottle in each side pocket. As an afterthought, I throw in a few spare batteries, even though with two lights plus my fully charged phone and my friends' phones, we should be perfectly fine.

"Eliza!" Claire calls up the stairs. "Your friends are here!"

"Coming!"

I put on my backpack, pocket my phone, and hurry down the stairs. Claire likes Meg just fine but she and Sherri do *not* get along. Claire's an introvert like me, but she's more . . . okay with it. She's been playing the piano since her fingers could fit on the keys, and she's going to University of North Texas on a full scholarship next year. She's a loner and it doesn't bother her and I admire it. The way she just goes for her goals and doesn't worry if she's missing part of the Teenage Experience because, as she told me once, *You don't miss something you don't want, Eliza.*

Sherri finds Claire's attitude *unhelpful.* She's always telling me I don't want to regret missing out on something, and the something I'll miss out on is not sitting in my room organizing rocks, apparently.

Claire gives me a thin-lipped smile. It's almost like looking at my own face. All three of us are red-haired and freckled— which is funny, since neither of our parents are—but Claire and I share the same shade of green eyes, the same long noses and oval faces.

"Be careful," she says, glancing at my friends, standing in the doorway. "You know what is and isn't a good idea. Don't let anyone convince you otherwise."

I heave an extremely large sigh.

"Yeah, got it, I know, I'm not Mom," Claire says. "But Mom's not home right now so I'm filling in."

I roll my eyes but smile because I know she means well. Claire's always taken it upon herself as oldest child to look after the rest of us. And Mara's taken it upon herself as youngest to test boundaries. I've never quite figured out what my own role is, to be honest.

"I'll be home by dinner," I tell her, and then I'm out the door with Sherri and Meg.

"What's the backpack for?" Sherri asks as the three of us get into her car. I'm in back, as usual, because Meg gets carsick.

"It's good to bring some stuff when you're going into an unfamiliar cave," I answer, buckling my seat belt and hugging the backpack protectively.

Meg and Sherri exchange a glance and I get a pit in my stomach. "What?"

"So we're definitely still going to the cave," Sherri answers quickly. "*Definitely*, because we promised. But we have to go somewhere else first."

"And where is that?" The pit grows.

"Drowners Swamp," says Meg.

"What? No *way*. Why would we do that?" I lean forward, gripping the back of Sherri's seat.

Sherri swats half-heartedly at my hand. "Don't distract me while I'm driving. We'll do your thing after! But Elijah Henlan said he'd pay fifty bucks if we take a selfie at the swamp."

"Where? Like, at the sign?"

"No." She rolls her eyes. "Next to the water."

She pulls off onto a dusty trailhead, less than half a mile from my house. We didn't need to make this drive; we could have walked. But I'm guessing Sherri didn't want to have this conversation within earshot of Claire.

"Sherri, this is beyond dumb. I thought—"

"Eliza, *please* can you not?" Meg interrupts. "I absolutely cannot handle the two of you fighting today. No one else in my life is allowed to be fighting right now."

I close my mouth at once. Meg gets upset pretty easily by arguing, and I can't blame her. She lives with her mom and her brother, both of whom are extremely manipulative. Her house is constant drama, and I can only imagine how exhausting it must be to live there. I try to always remember and respect that, and make her life easier where I can.

"You promise we're going to the cave after?" I say, breaking a very long silence.

Sherri twists around in her seat. "I promise."

"Then . . . I guess we can do this."

Sherri and Meg open their car doors in unison, and my fingertips start tingling unpleasantly. My gut tells me I was just played, but I don't know how to get out of this. My friendship with Meg has had its ups and downs over the years, but it's always felt comfortable. Until Sherri came into the picture, replacing comfort with adventure, and leaving me wondering where I fit. Middle sister, middle friend. Wherever I go, I'm kind of stuck.

I hop out of the car, shouldering my backpack. I almost

leave it behind, but honestly, I'm more likely to need a first-aid kit here than in a cave. By the time I shut my door, they're already walking well ahead of me. Easy and comfortable, like *they're* the ones who've been friends since grade school. I rush to catch up, feeling sick.

Living within walking distance to a swamp, there's one thing my parents impressed upon my sisters and me more than anything else: *Don't* go near it.

The ominously named Drowners Swamp isn't particularly huge. And we don't have the same dangerous swamp creatures here in Upstate New York that you might find in, say, Florida. No alligator will pop out and chew off my arm. But the ground's unstable and there are snakes. Reason enough, in my opinion, to stay far, far away.

The walk isn't too long, and mostly it follows the hiking trail we parked at the base of. But once we veer off into less traveled territory, I can hear my mom's voice echoing in my head with every step: *Do not go to that swamp, Eliza. People die there.*

"How sure are we about the fifty dollars?" I ask. "And why does he even want you to do this?"

Sherri shrugs. She's ahead of me, so I can't see her face when she says, "Elijah's weird. And we're sure he will pay because I will *make* him."

She won't, is the thing. Sherri can say that Elijah's weird all she wants, but she will do pretty much anything he suggests. Or, at least, she'll *appear* to do it.

I don't like the bitter edge to all my thoughts about my two best friends right now. I love them both, but as our sophomore year has gone on, they've gotten closer and I've started to feel like I'm trying to hold water in clenched fists every time I'm with them.

Meg's quiet, which means she's brooding about something, which means she wants me to ask. So I do.

Her response is a twist of her hair around a finger, and a slow-moving frown. "Everything's fine," she says. "Mom's just commenting on my eating habits again."

Immediately, I'm aglow with rage. "Seriously? You eat fine."

"I know." She folds her arms tight. "But you know how she is. I'm up two pounds and the world is ending, basically."

"I wish you could just come stay at my house," I say.

"Or mine," Sherri adds quickly. Then, with a glance and a small smile at me, she says, "We could trade you."

Meg laughs. "Well, just over two more years until you guys can fight over who gets to room with me at college."

"Be warned," Sherri says to me, "I plan to win that fight."

"Yeah, you wish," I say, even though we both know that if it comes down to it, she *will* win. She always does.

"So tell me about this cave we're gonna go to," says Sherri.

I narrow my eyes at the back of her head. Whenever she shows a slight interest in anything geology-related and I take the bait, it always seems to find a way of coming back to haunt me.

"Claire and I found it last weekend when we were hiking. We didn't really go in, but we went far enough to tell that no bears or anything live there, and that it goes on for a little ways. I'm hoping it has some interesting formations."

"Um, bears?" Meg says delicately.

"Bears live in caves sometimes. I feel like you already know that."

"I guess I never really thought about it."

"Don't worry." I pick at a nail. "There definitely weren't any around."

Sherri edges carefully around a very overgrown raspberry bush. I follow her, and then stop. Here we are. Drowners Swamp.

It doesn't look like much. Just a bunch of grasses and flowers and scraggly trees leading up to a narrow body of water. The water has some grass clumps sticking out here and there, too, and scattered dead trees. Next to me stands a big sign that reads *DANGER!!!*—an excellent reminder of exactly why I didn't want to be here. Mom's disapproving voice no longer echoes quietly in my head; now it's practically a scream. I picture the newspaper articles she's been forcing in front of our noses since birth, every time something bad happens here.

"We shouldn't do this," I say. "We're gonna get eaten by something."

Sherri scoffs. "No, we aren't. When was the last time anything bad happened here? What even lives here that could hurt us?"

I don't have a good answer. People don't come to this swamp unless they're idiots like us. The ground is prone to sinkholes. Deep ones.

And it's nice that Sherri's able to forget poisonous snakes exist, but I'm all too aware. As much as I like nature, I could do without the snakes.

My eyes sweep over the ground before me. The center of the swamp, with its crystal clear, still water and dead tree trunks. The rim of bright green algae around the water's edges, and the lumpy, grass-tufted area extending between there and here. We shouldn't even be this close. It's not like wild animals respect boundary signs and leave you alone till you pass one.

"I don't know when the last time anyone got bit by a snake here was," I say carefully. Sherri asked the question, but I keep my eyes on Meg, who's my better bet if I want this called off. "But someone did supposedly get pulled into a sinkhole, like, three years ago."

Meg's mouth is a thin, silent line, but Sherri rolls her eyes. "Well, you wanted to see a cave. Aren't you the one who believes that ridiculous urban legend about this place?"

I should have known she would throw that in my face. I love that urban legend because it's weird and it's cave-themed, not because I actually *believe* it. If I did, I would run.

The myth is kind of a *Journey to the Center of the Earth*–type situation. The reality is that a lot of people have disappeared over the years, usually under mysterious circumstances. According to legend, when you disappear, you find some tunnel that leads deep into the earth. Like, all the way in.

Being a total geology nerd, I know how ridiculous that is.

No, let me rephrase: Being a human over the age of ten, I know how ridiculous that is.

You wouldn't get too far before you'd melt like a marshmallow over a fire pit.

But that's beside the point.

"You know that's made up," I say quietly. "And you know this isn't smart."

Sherri glances out at the swamp, and for the first time, I notice a hint of something like fear in her eyes. I can tell that Meg notices it, too. "It isn't the *smartest*," Sherri admits. "But I already said I'd do it. You know I don't back down."

I don't say anything else. It's futile. Especially after she and Meg exchange a look, one that tells me they've discussed things without me. I fold my arms to squeeze against the bad feeling growing bigger in my stomach.

"If we're going to do this, then let's go," Meg says. "No point standing here by this stupid sign."

Sherri tosses her mane of dark brown hair and takes a step forward. Meg and I follow quickly; it's best not to be left in Sherri's dust. They're both wearing boots, and I'm wearing sneakers. It did not occur to me that my footwear wouldn't be ideal here. Mainly because we weren't supposed to be here in the first place. Of course, *their* footwear would be totally inappropriate in a cave. Which, I suppose, is telling.

The toe of Sherri's boot catches in the gap between two roots of a scraggly tree, and she wraps her hand around the narrow trunk with a small cry. I freeze, listening in case she startled anything that might eat us.

"My boot's stuck," she says, tugging.

"I'll help you." Meg crouches beside her. "Eliza, you go on."

"*What?*" I fold my arms again. "No way. I'll wait."

"Just go," Sherri says exasperatedly. "You're the one who knows about sinkholes and crap, so you're the one who can avoid them. Find us a good path."

"You can't tell where one is." My voice snaps with impatience. "That's what makes them so terrifying."

"We'll be right behind you in a sec," Meg says. "Don't be a wimp."

The tingling in my fingertips is getting worse, which happens to me a lot when I face confrontation, especially with my friends. I don't want them mad at me, freezing me out. The feeling is pretty much always an indicator that my anxiety has reached levels where it's easier to give in. So I give in.

"Fine." I turn away from them, settle my eyes on the water. And I start toward it, watching the ground for signs of instability. Problem is, it all looks unstable. The ground is muddy and oozing between grass tufts.

Swamp plants and algae squish wetly beneath my feet as I carefully traverse the terrain, edging closer to the deepest part of the swamp, the water, where deadly snakes are probably waiting in hoards. Cold water seeps through my sneakers, shocking my toes. I glance behind me, at my friends.

Sherri doesn't look like she's trying too hard to free her foot, and I'm starting to get the unpleasant feeling that I sometimes get, that they're secretly laughing at me.

"Go *on*!" Sherri shouts.

The knot in my stomach burns. I press a hand to my waist, like that'll help.

This is much worse than Sherri's usual ideas. I could be killed, and for what? I'll deal with whatever mocking ensues; Elijah's fifty dollars is not worth my life. I turn carefully, back toward them, trying not to ruin my shoes.

Three steps later, the ground collapses. The space beneath my feet is suddenly empty. My body lurches and I grab for anything my fists can grip. My fingers snag around a broken root and I cling to it with all the strength I possess, holding my upper body above the surface.

My eyes lock with Meg's. Hers are wide with horror. Sherri's foot isn't stuck anymore.

I reach for the root with my other hand, but it's slick with mud and my grasp slips. The world goes silent except for the sound of blood pounding in my ears. My muscles tremble with the effort of holding on. The walls of this gaping hole are too slippery for me to get a foothold. My hands slide farther down the root, and there's nothing else to grab.

Time stops. My stomach flips inside out. This root is all that stands between me and death. And I'm nearly at its end.

2

Then the silence breaks—Meg screams and starts toward me, a couple of running steps before Sherri grabs her and pulls her back.

"You'll fall, too!" Sherri shouts. "We have to go get someone."

It's true; it isn't safe. But they're my only hope.

"Please!" I shout, my voice cracking.

The root snaps. Just after I speak. It rips free of the earth with a shower of dirt, and then I'm free-falling into nothing. My hands claw, my feet kick. A long scream escapes my lips. I bounce and tumble and then slam back-first onto solid ground, the contents of my bag stabbing my spine. The wind goes out of me, abruptly cutting off the scream; I cough and gasp.

Then dirt trickles onto my face. Faster and faster.

I pull myself to sit, back into one of the dirt walls in the space around me, and look up, a hand shielding my eyes.

I'm in a hole. A deep hole, judging by the pinprick of light above me. A sinkhole.

A glob of mud slops onto the ground beside me. Another

lands on my knee. Dirt and debris join it, all raining down, gathering speed.

"Help," I whimper. Then, much louder, "Meg, Sherri, *help!*"

A desperate shout comes from somewhere above. I don't know which of my friends the horrified sound belongs to. It's no use, though. The dirt's going to bury me alive before anyone can save me.

I take quick stock of my surroundings. The hole is almost perfectly cylindrical, and I think if I stretched out on my back, I could touch one end with my toes and the other with my finger-tips. Its walls aren't solid enough for me to grab on to and climb—I try, but fail, and mud slops down, huge globs narrow-ing the walls as they fall. Maybe, if it fills slowly enough, I can stay on top of the mud. Ride it back to the surface. Maybe my friends will run really fast and find someone before I suffocate.

But I know in my heart that isn't going to happen.

Too easily, I picture myself covered, the muck pressing into my mouth, onto my body. Dying, knowing all the while exactly what's happening to me. The mud is not closing in slowly anymore.

I crawl, desperately, around the edges of the hole. The side opposite me slopes downward a bit, like it feeds into something.

It does.

An even smaller hole, edges dripping with clay. This hole wouldn't exist if it didn't lead somewhere, I feel sure of it.

I don't hesitate because I don't have a choice. I throw myself into the opening. I fit, but barely. My arms scrape the sides, and

I have to writhe forward almost snakelike. The hole narrows more as the slope steepens. I dig my toes into the clay and push. I have to stretch my arms up in front of me and wriggle, and still my shoulders only fit because the soil is so loose. This will either end up the best or worst decision I could have made.

Dirt and clay push behind me; if this tunnel doesn't open to somewhere big, I'm going to end up just as dead as if I'd stayed in the sinkhole where I fell. I can't think about that.

I keep shoving, jerking my body forward like the world's most uncoordinated fish. It gets more and more difficult and I realize that I may actually have to come to terms with not making it through. With the slow, horrifying death of suffocation. I consider how to end things quicker, but I can't move well enough to reach the pocketknife in my backpack. Not that a pocketknife would necessarily give me a better death, anyway.

With an explosion of dirt and clay, I finally burst free—free-falling again, that is. My limbs flail and then, with sharp echoes of pain in my hip and skull, I hit the ground. I flex and twist carefully, making sure nothing's broken before I back away from the thinning waterfall of dirt that followed me into this larger, pitch-black space.

Everything seems okay, other than a gentle throbbing at the back of my head, some general soreness, and a deep ache in my ears. I roll my jaw, and my ears pop, lessening the ache.

The all-consuming blackness makes me uneasy, though. It presses like weights on my eyes. I dig around in my clay-slicked backpack for my cell phone. My trembling fingers can barely close around the device, and my heart sinks when I turn it on to no service. I dig deeper into the backpack for my flashlight and my headlamp, using both of those along with my phone's flashlight to send beams around me in multiple directions, trying to figure out what kind of place this is. Whether I'm safe—at least for now.

I'm in a cavern. Medium-sized, with high walls and three different tunnels branching off it. The walls seem to be mostly made of rock, and in a few places they drip with condensation. Something to remember for later, if I run out of water. I take a deep breath, running all these facts through my mind to keep calm.

Once I know the place doesn't present me with any immediate dangers, I take a second lap around the cave, slower. I stop at the entrances to each tunnel and investigate. One blows back the red strands of my hair with a gentle breeze, which feels great since it's humid and sticky down here. Warmer than normal, unless I'm much deeper in the earth than I'd expect.

It's actually a beautiful cavern. Clusters of flowstone that look like jellyfish with long, dangling tentacles. Soda straws spiking jaggedly from the ceiling. Helictite bush formations in the shape of dendritic trees. And so much more. I've explored as many caves as my parents have allowed me to, and this one ranks near the top.

But I'm trapped. Which really sucks the joy out of the situation.

I sit with my back against a thick, twisted stalagmite,

and . . . do nothing. I shiver despite the warmth, uncomfortable in my damp, clay-coated clothing. Probably I should be panicking, but I'm calm. Staring around like a queen on her throne, threading my fingers absently through the strap on my backpack. I'm glad I have my few supplies, at least. I didn't prepare for a cave like *this*, but I did prepare for a cave.

On a whim, I dig through, pull out the notebook, and start scribbling. Maybe it's deeply morbid, but I think I should record what happened to me. In case I don't make it. In case someone finds my body, and then maybe they'll know.

I'll make my way back to the surface. That's what I'm telling myself, anyway, and I've never wanted to believe anything so badly. But still. Having a record of how I perished, just in case, seems practical.

So I sit, hunched over my notebook, and tell myself everything is going to be fine, even if writing these words might be the last thing I do.

After my brief rest, I explore the cave a bit more, admiring its features and taking notes in my new journal. I even manage to clean myself up a bit, stripping naked and using the water that trickles down one wall to wash my clothes and skin as best I can. They don't dry well in the humidity and darkness, but at least I brought something to change into.

I feel better. And honestly I felt pretty wild getting totally undressed in the middle of a wide-open cave, even if there's a zero percent chance anyone will walk in on me. Nudity is nudity, and I'm the kind of girl who changes in a bathroom stall rather than face the mind-numbing terror of doing it in front of others and pretending I don't care what they think about the shape of my body.

First, I check out the two least promising tunnels branching off the cavern. They're both total dead air. One curves upward, but ends in a pile of rocks almost immediately. The other slopes steeply downward. I don't go too far. The air is thick with moisture, the floor slippery with condensation. I picture myself tumbling till I smash my head open on a rock wall somewhere even farther below.

The tunnel with the breeze feels like my only hope. I'm banking pretty hard on it. And I've procrastinated going in because I'm utterly terrified at the thought that it might *not* lead me out.

I'm not usually claustrophobic, but right now I'm not feeling so good about how narrow this tunnel is. I have to turn sideways in spots, and it makes the breath hitch in my lungs. The anxiety is familiar, but it's usually people who make me feel like this.

The only thing that eases my fear is the upward tilt of the tunnel's rough floor. I mean, the tilt is slight. But it's there.

I'm using only the headlamp for now; it's easier to move if I'm not carrying something in my hands. But I can't see very well, even in the sharp white of its LED bulbs, and keep banging my elbows when the path twists sharply in a new direction. I think I'm bleeding, but I don't want to stop and look. I'm not a fan of blood.

When the tunnel's slope changes to what can only be described as *downward*, I try not to think about it. It's only temporary, I tell myself. I don't want it to lead upward too fast, anyway, do I? Drowning in a swamp isn't really how I want this to end.

And not to make light of the situation, but I can*not* be betrayed like this by caves. I've been obsessed with caves since I can remember. Caves and rocks and the earth.

It's weird, Meg always tells me—at least, she has recently. *No one wants to listen to you go on about rocks, Eliza.*

So I don't go on about them. Not out loud, anyway. But I read endlessly and I've made my parents take me to basically every cave in the state of New York that you're allowed to visit, and I can't imagine *anything* else I would rather do with my life than study how the earth works.

I trip over what feels like a brittle stick. It snaps beneath my foot, and I manage to stay upright. Bracing myself against the wall, I angle my headlamp downward.

It's a skeleton.

A human skeleton.

How did I get talked into this? I keep asking myself that. And I mean, I know how. It was Sherri, it's always Sherri. She legit has the worst ideas of anyone I've ever met, but she says them with such authority. Such conviction. And somehow, the fallout of her ideas is always worse for me than for her or Meg. I don't know. That's probably not true. Except this time.

Next time Sherri has a terrible idea, I'm gonna say no. I don't care if she and Meg laugh when I say, "Isn't that dangerous?" Because nothing bad ever happens to them.

Only to me.

3

I scream.

It echoes off the walls, pierces the blackness in front of me, ringing far into the distance.

I'm immediately embarrassed by my reaction, even though no one's around. It's only a skeleton. Nothing alive. Still, however irrational, my heart clutches my throat in a stranglehold. My limbs have turned to dust.

The skeleton has been here a long, long while. I scattered a few bones—the thing that crunched under my foot was a piece of leg—but whoever these remains once belonged to stopped here, sat with their back against one wall and their feet against the other, and just . . . gave up. The skull grins wickedly at me, like it knows I'm next. I can't get over how *empty* it is. Not a shred of clothing remaining, not a wisp of hair or a hint of flesh.

I glance down at the stark white fingers, folded primly into the lap, and I imagine that this skeleton is me. That I've lost all hope of escape, and I've sat down someplace to die. I shudder. It has *not* been long enough to let my brain start wandering dark paths. I'll be fine. I *will* find an exit.

With a great force of will, I tear my gaze from the skeleton and hurry on my way. I *have* to get out of here. I won't be the girl who stops moving and gives up. I'm not confident about a lot of things, but I *am* confident about the earth and caves and geology. I can do this.

I drag a hand along the surface of the wall. The cool stone beneath my fingers doesn't bring me any relief. Despite my attempts to give myself a pep talk, this is when it hits me, finally, how *trapped* I am. Rock is so solid, so unyielding. I'm starting to get that panic tingle in my limbs. The only thing that keeps me from breaking down is walking. The slope steepens, and the tunnel narrows, but I pretend that neither of those things are true. I've been in tons of caves where you have to slip sideways between jagged walls, or crawl on hands and knees to get under a low ceiling. I always thought it was fun.

But now as I shuffle sideways, my stomach sucked into my ribs, it doesn't feel so fun. Which frustrates me, because this is an incredibly neat cave system. That cavern back there with all its beautiful formations, and this tunnel with all its twists . . . it's everything I love.

If only I hadn't stumbled on some major evidence that it might not have an exit.

But I tell myself there's no way to know what happened to the person whose skeleton that was. It looks like they probably just gave up too soon.

I lose track of time, squeezing, crawling, climbing. The tunnel opens up, and suddenly, I'm in another cavern.

It's taller than the last one; I can't see the ceiling, even when I add my cell phone's light to my headlamp's. I was hoping for service here, but still nothing.

This cavern is a maze of formations. Stalagmites and stalactites interlocking like the teeth of a predator. There are chandeliers and columns and draperies. Frostwork and moonmilk and cave popcorn.

I weave through, claws of anxiety kneading my stomach as I go deeper into the room without finding any tunnels. Is this a dead end? It can't be. Can't.

I reach water, and this is what breaks me. An underground lake. Water completely unmoving. No visible tunnels.

Totally trapped.

I curl into a ball at the water's edge and let my tears free. It's been a few hours now. My feet are sore, my whole *body* is sore. I'm hungry and tired and I want to go home.

What are Sherri and Meg doing right now? Did they tell my sisters where we went? Does everyone know that I'm missing? Has anyone called my parents? My friends must think I'm dead. There's no other conclusion, and I bet they're freaking out. Sherri gets pretty mad when I mess up her plans. I try not to, but I wasn't born with whatever it is that makes people reckless. I fake it the best I can, but she knows I'm not really brave. Everyone knows.

I'm so much happier sitting in my room, poring over books

about rocks. Not sneaking out to parties on weekends after my parents are asleep. Not stealing candy from the local convenience store. Not wandering around dangerous swamps.

But I say yes to all of it, because without Sherri and Meg, I don't know how to have the experiences I'm supposed to be having, and I don't want to be a weirdo loner no one will talk to. Which is what Sherri says I'm turning into.

I'm terrified she's right.

My hand slips into the water when I move to push myself upright, and it surprises me. It's . . . *hot*. I sit up quickly, dipping my fingers back into the liquid. It feels like a sauna. Interesting.

I shine my phone's flashlight over the surface of the water. It's incredibly clear, but I can't see a bottom. Steam rises lazily from the still pool. I bite my lip, thinking.

If the cave is as closed off as it seems, there could conceivably be prehistoric life in this lake. Most likely microbes, because I don't see any fish, but who knows how deep this thing goes. Could be anything.

I read about these microscopic creatures once, tardigrades. They can live in extreme environments—temperature, pressure, radiation, all of that. Some even survived an experiment where they were exposed to outer freaking space. They can dehydrate themselves and basically put their lives on pause for decades with no food or water. That's the kind of thing I figure resides in this place. Maybe some cavefish, and if I'm not confused, there aren't any species of cavefish that would attack a human. Nothing scarier than that should be in this water.

I hope I'm not wrong about that.

Because what I'm about to do is completely counter to my not-reckless nature.

I'm going to swim across this lake.

Best speleothems I've seen so far:

* Helictite bushes in the first cavern. Most of them were pretty small, but a couple were taller than me. They're all spiky and wild shaped, yet somehow so delicate. I didn't dare touch one for fear of snapping off a branch.

* Moonmilk. There's a bunch of it to my left right now. I touched it. It felt cottage cheesy. A little gross, but also cool.

* A flowstone formation that looked like a perfect archway. When I was about halfway across this cavern, I stopped to look at it. I didn't walk beneath it, though, because it looked kinda precarious.

4

Swimming across this lake is not as easy as I was anticipating. It's fortunate that I thought to bring a headlamp, but the darkness in a cavern is so indescribably complete that my bobbing stripe of light doesn't help as much as I'd like.

I strip down to my underwear again after a long debate with myself—ultimately concluding that if someone finds me dead, it won't matter what I'm wearing. I leave the clothes next to my backpack on the shore.

Fingers crossed nothing takes a bite out of me.

I slide in carefully. The water is deep right away; I can't touch bottom. The warmth soothes some of my aches. Eases the soreness in my back and hip from my earlier fall. Loosens the tension in my muscles.

The beam of my flashlight bounces off the surface. It doesn't show me much, but at least I'll know before I run into a wall.

Something brushes against my foot. I squeeze my eyes shut for a moment.

"Please do not eat me," I say to whatever it is, holding as utterly still as I can while keeping afloat.

It doesn't. I let out a long, slow breath and keep swimming.

I swim beneath a low ceiling. The air is foggy under here, and has that musty scent of a place long untouched. I breathe deep, hold it in my lungs. I love that smell.

On the other side of the low ceiling, I emerge into another room.

"Thank God," I say aloud, breathlessly. Not sure it's a good sign that I've started talking to myself.

The lake ends here on what I'm going to call a "beach," using the term super loosely. But there's actually a bank; my feet touch rough, rocky bottom. This place is like a steam room, much smaller than the cavern on the other side and swirling with mist. Condensation drips from the ceiling.

I direct myself toward a spot that feels almost chilly, and find a narrow opening in the wall. Another tunnel.

My heart soars. An exit.

But a descending one.

It's starting to worry me, much as I try to tell myself otherwise. Something about this cavern feels very . . . *off.* I'm standing here, dripping, in my underwear, and I'm not cold. My body feels strange in an indefinable way, and so does my mind, really. Why am I anxious about things I'm not usually anxious about, like confined spaces? And simultaneously calm about this whole thing?

It's probably nothing. But now that I'm mulling it over, questions jostle each other, racing through my brain.

I turn away from the tunnel and swim back to where I left my things. I need to move on before I start to panic. Because panic feels imminent.

But then, as I'm stuffing my clothes into my backpack, I pause to think for a minute. The thing is, I'm exhausted. My body's running on adrenaline alone, and it's taken a serious beating today. That tunnel isn't going anywhere, and the thought of staying here for a little bit is pretty inviting.

My stomach hurts, thinking about what must be going on above the surface. Guilt at making everyone wait while I rest weighs heavy on my shoulders. Getting back to the surface should be my first priority. I get dressed and sit at the water's edge, legs dangling into the warm, buoyant liquid. I never imagined myself in a situation like this. My parents have always been a bit wary about my cave stuff, but I'm a cautious person, and they trust me. We had protocols in place. I never wavered.

Until today. However accidental.

My parents must know by now. No matter how freaked out Sherri and Meg were, even if they thought they'd be blamed for what happened, they would have gone for help right away. My parents are probably home, believing I'm dead. Claire's probably told them how she warned me to be careful because even though it's a totally inappropriate thing to say at this moment in time, she never can stop herself. When I get home, I'll let her scream it in my face.

Sherri and Meg pressured me into this, but they didn't physically force me. I did this to my family, all on my own. How would I feel if something happened to Claire or Mara? I'm so ashamed of myself.

My mom's a worrier. She's the one who stood, wringing her hands, while my dad put us on bikes without training wheels for the first time. Who wouldn't let us go too high on the swings. Who put the fear of God into me about pregnancy the moment I started my period.

I don't want to think about what this will do to her. After all her warnings, all her attempts to turn me into a girl who thinks before she acts, who uses caution and not impulsivity, I ended up like this anyway.

We're a close-knit family, always have been. Mom's a farm manager and Dad's a contractor. They both work long, weird hours, but they're around when we need them. Meg's always telling me my life's charmed, my family's perfect. That I can never understand what it means to have something bad happen in my life because I'm shielded from it all.

Guess I proved *her* wrong.

What if I don't make it home is the thought that keeps cycling through my head. I'm trying to suppress it, because it's so awful. *It'll be so easy for them to go on without me* is another awful thought. I'm just sort of *there*, in the middle. Mara and Claire can close in, fill the space I used to occupy.

They'll all be sad at first, sure. But they'll get used to life without me.

I don't know. Maybe that's comforting.

I stand abruptly, because sitting here wallowing isn't helping me at all. Rest seemed like a good idea, but now I think it's just increasing my panic. I adjust my headlamp and shoulder my backpack. A thorough sweep of the room's perimeter seems like a good idea, before I take the downward-sloping tunnel. A gentle breeze blows through here, which makes me wonder if I missed another tunnel hidden behind cave formations somewhere.

I get out my flashlight because as much as I appreciate my headlamp, I can't swing it abruptly to look at something off to the side without a sharp turn of my neck, and it's feeling pretty jarred and achy from my fall. I like the way the flashlight cuts a line through the darkness. The dark has never particularly frightened me. In caves, especially, I like how everything is kept in shadow except whatever you're aiming a light at. You're focused on the path ahead, or truly appreciating the beauty of whatever formation you're investigating, not distracted by other sights in your periphery. I know there could be bad things hiding in the shadows, but I guess maybe my brain is too busy feeling anxious about people to understand when it should be anxious about something else.

It seems like I'm not going to find anything. Until I sweep my flashlight to the left, toward the middle part of the cavern, and I catch a flash of white. I stop dead.

It's another skeleton.

This one sits with its back against a stalagmite, hands folded primly in its lap, just like the last one I saw. It still has a bit of flesh clinging to the bone in some places, a few remaining wisps of long hair glued to its skull, but once again, not a single scrap of clothing.

My heart accelerates. It struck me as odd last time, but this time it strikes me as ominous. Flesh should decompose much faster than clothing. Or shoes, especially shoes. And why do people keep dying in this position? Sitting casually, happily, like they're totally at peace with their last breath. How often does that happen? Maybe once, but definitely not twice.

I back away from the skeleton, bumping into a thick pillar hard enough that it nearly knocks the wind from me. Something is not right in this place, and suddenly, I'm struck with a terrible, terrible thought.

Maybe I'm not alone down here.

There actually is a passageway that I missed, I discover, after I've semi-calmed from the skeleton incident. A thin fissure in the wall, so narrow I have to remove my backpack and hold it dangling from my fingertips, yet still barely manage to squeeze through. I exhale and suck in my stomach, which makes me feel panicked and out of breath. But my brain whispers over and over, *You can go back if it gets smaller you can go back you can go back*, and, thankfully, the tunnel widens.

Widens, and slopes *up*.

My relief is so potent that my limbs get heavy while my head gets dizzy. I press my flashlight-free hand to the ever-surprisingly warm, clammy wall to steady myself, and keep going. Ahead, I see what must be light. It has a bit of a bluish, neonish quality, but sunlight always looks a little strange to me when I've been in the dark for a while. I pause to stow my flashlight because the headlamp is enough as the light ahead grows stronger.

My parents are going to be so angry with me but also so thankful and so *relieved*. I will take whatever punishment they offer up, even if I'm grounded from now until the end of high school. I just want to be out of here; I've never wanted out of a cave so badly in my life. Maybe I'll come back someday, on purpose, through an entrance that is not a sinkhole in the swamp. And not alone, either.

Something moves up ahead. The *light* moves. The light—it isn't the sun, I realize, heart sinking all the way to my feet. It's . . . a solid form, a humanlike form. A glowing human? I can't make sense of what I'm seeing, but what I *can* make sense of is that it looks like it's holding a weapon and it seems to be heading toward me.

Run, my instincts tell me.

So I run.

Some basic cave safety practices I've been following for years.

* Always tell someone where you're going and (approximately) when you'll be back

* If you get lost or hurt or lose your light, stay and wait for help

* Remain calm

* Know your limits and don't push them

* Don't run

* Never, N E V E R go caving alone

Today I have broken every single one of these rules.

5

All I can think about is getting back to the water, getting across and through to the tunnel on the other side. When I reach the lake's edge, I glance back. The tunnel I just fled emits a faint glow, which sets my heart racing. I grab my backpack and slip into the water as silently as I can, holding my backpack aloft in one hand while I swim.

Everything's quiet except my harsh breathing and the gentle ripple of water with each stroke of my arm. Everything's dark except the thin beam of light cut by my headlamp. The darkness doesn't feel soothing anymore, or the quiet. It was one thing when I figured nothing else was here. Now the dark and quiet seem sinister. Dangerous.

Of course, apparently, so is the light.

On the other side of the low-hanging wall, I slip through the crack to another passageway, wishing I had time to change my sopping wet clothes. The tunnel's narrow and downward sloping and the floor is slippery. Not ideal. Its sharp turns disorient me. I don't like this at all, don't want to be heading deeper into this already too-warm cave. My lungs and my head still feel a little wrong, and I think it must be changes in the air pressure, which is something I've never experienced. Caves I've visited don't get deep enough for these kinds of side effects. I didn't even know you *could* get deep enough for effects like that, to be honest.

I glance behind me, half expecting to see a glow shimmering in the air. But there's nothing. My pace slows, and I start to doubt what I saw. If I saw anything. When people are lost in the desert, they see mirages, right? I've never wanted to see daylight so badly, maybe my brain manufactured it, except my brain can never just be kind to me, so it turned the sunlight into something more sinister.

The breeze in this passageway comforts me, if only slightly. If there's a breeze, there's airflow. And airflow can only be a good thing. Even if the descending slope of the tunnel causes anxiety to claw at my gut. I think longingly of the other tunnel, the one that was actually an incline, and wonder if I should go back.

The memory of the glowing human form frightens me enough to keep me from trying it, though. Especially when combined with the memory of the neatly seated skeletons, stripped of their clothes.

Around a bend, the tunnel branches into two forks. They're basically identical, and I freeze with indecision.

Until I hear what can only be described as a growl emanating from the left fork.

I don't know what made the growl, what could possibly live down here that makes a sound like that, but I don't want to be anywhere near it.

Right fork it is, then. I can't rush, because the floor is still slippery and damp, and the downward tilt has become tiltier. But I don't want the growling thing to catch up to me, either.

My heartbeat thrums in my fingertips as I move along, feeling like Red Riding Hood pursued by the wolf. I glance over my shoulder and see nothing, but my headlamp aims mostly at the wall when I do that, so it's all just oppressive darkness anyway.

An uneven spot catches my toe and I stumble. My nails scrape the walls and one tears with a burst of pain.

I'm not proud of the word that slips from my mouth when it happens.

Or the one I say when the headlamp flies off, clatters to the ground, and flickers out. My phone and my flashlight are still in my backpack, but this headlamp is so much easier; I *need* it.

I edge carefully forward on my knees, sweeping one arm in front of me to feel for the light. My breathing is so loud, the only noise in this narrow space. It echoes behind me as I—

That's not an echo.

I'm not the only thing breathing in this space.

I give up on the headlamp, reach into my bag, and find my cell phone. It's off, and my heart hammers while a numb-fingered hand presses the power button, aiming the screen behind me. The glow as it turns itself on reflects off something.

Eyes.

The eyes of a predator.

I scream, and run. My toe collides with the headlamp and I hear it bounce ahead of me. I'm sightless, grazing myself on the walls, praying there's not a sudden turn ahead that I smack head-long into. The creature snarls at my back, chasing me now, obviously, because I'm an idiot who fled.

I didn't get a good look at it, so I don't know how big it is or how dangerous, but if it can see and I can't, the answer to the latter is probably *very*.

My foot slips on the ever-steepening, condensation-heavy floor and I tumble forward. Keep tumbling, completely out of control.

And then I'm soaring, and the air around me glows orange. For a moment, I wonder if this is the end, if I'm going to heaven.

Then I slam into solid ground with a burst of indescribable pain, and the orange glow seems more like fire.

If I'm going anywhere now, it's hell.

I might be the only person in the world whose personal hero is named Etheldred. Etheldred Benett, to be more specific. This kinda veers from the topic of me and this cave situation, but I'm thinking about her right now. Most people have never heard of Etheldred, but she's considered the first "lady geologist." She even got an honorary doctorate from the University of St. Petersburg, despite the fact that women were not admitted there. It only happened because Tsar Nicholas I thought, based on her name, that she was a man, but still. She earned it. It wasn't her fault he was an idiot.

Etheldred was a fossil collector and that's not my thing, but she was important during a time when women were openly considered lesser. When I feel like I don't know what I'm doing, like my goals are ridiculous and I'll never achieve them, like I'm the most nothing person in the entire world, I think of her and everything she accomplished.

I'll never have her courage, it's not who I am. But she inspires me to try.

6

The creature comes shooting out after me, snarling and spitting. It lands a few feet away with a yelp, then leaps immediately to its feet. It's worse, now that I can see the doglike thing in this orange light. It has colorless fur and pink eyes. About the size of a large fox, but it's much more solid, with thicker legs and a broader chest. Its ears slick back against its head and drool oozes from its sneering mouth.

I curl into myself, because I can't get up. Something's broken and it hurts so much. The animal knows it's got me beat. It saunters toward me, all casual, while I whimper and try to edge away—and fail, because I can barely breathe.

With a whistle of air, something lodges in the throat of the creature. It falters and gasps, blood pouring from its neck, drooling from its mouth in ribbons. It lets out a few choking gurgles and slumps to the ground.

I look in the direction the arrow came from. The direction where the orange glow is strongest, and I see . . . *people.*

A boy my age, bow still raised, is silhouetted by flickering firelight behind him. His brow is furrowed, he's almost scowling, but he looks pleased with himself, too.

Behind him, others have gathered, and I start to freak out. How did they get here? Who are they?

Maybe the dog-creature wasn't the worst thing I had to worry about.

I curl even further into myself and start crying.

A woman crouches at my side, gently touching my arm. "It's all right," she says, her voice soft and soothing. Her gray-tinged hair and hazel eyes remind me of my mom.

"Is it?" I ask faintly. The pain makes it hard to breathe. I don't want to consider that I might be dying, but this seems like a bad sign.

"Did you hit your head?" she asks.

"I don't think so. Maybe a little, I mean, I hit everything. But it doesn't hurt. I can't . . . I can't breathe very well, though."

"Maybe you've broken a rib." She smooths the hair away from my face and I wonder if she has a teenage daughter of her own, or if she's just nurturing with everyone. "But don't worry. You're safe here, and we'll get you all healed up."

I want to believe her, but I can't make my heart stop racing. "Where am I?"

She bites her lip and stops touching my hair. "We call this the colony. A home for those of us who've been lost to this cave over the years."

A pit opens up in my stomach. "How did . . . how did you end up here?" A tiny cough escapes my lips. Breathing hurts, talking hurts. Coughing hurts the most.

"We can talk about this later," she says. "I should check out your injuries before you get yourself too worked up."

"No," I insist, even though the strength of my voice stabs into my bones. "I want to know."

"I fell into a vertical shaft on a walk in the woods. Wandered around for a while, eventually ended up here. Everyone's got a similar story."

"Did anyone get dropped underground by a sinkhole?"

"That one isn't common, but believe it or not, yes."

I thought that'd make me feel better. It doesn't.

"This is a lot to absorb," she says. "I don't think now is the time."

"How long have you been here?" I press.

She pauses. Then, "Six years."

The pit in my stomach envelops my entire body. "Okay," I whisper. "I guess I'm done asking questions for now."

She smiles understandingly and I wonder how many times she's had this exact same conversation.

And whether anyone who's come into this place—this *colony*—has ever left.

The woman's name is Colleen, and she's the unofficial doctor for the group. She was a nurse before ending up here, and the only one with any medical training whatsoever.

"I don't know *everything* a doctor does," she said with a wry smile, "but I know enough. And some things they don't."

Thank God for it, too. Because it turns out that I definitely have at least one bruised or possibly broken rib, in addition to my other, more minor aches and pains.

I wish I could say that I'm taking this all in stride. That I've overcome my injured ribs and integrated with the group immediately.

But I have not. Not even a little.

The pain is unlike anything I've experienced before. It's a thousand shards of hot metal poking into my lung every time I inhale. Colleen says I have to keep trying to breathe normally, though, for the benefit of my lungs. She sets me up in a big tent made of a stiff, semi-foul-smelling material that I think is the hide of some animal, and lit only by the faint glow of firelight coming from outside it, which means barely lit at all. I lie flat on my back atop a cot that looks like something you might use while camping. It's definitely not handmade.

Colleen stays in the tent for a while, fussing over me, smoothing my hair. I try not to cry because she's a stranger and I want to be brave. And more important, because crying *hurts*. I ask a lot of questions to distract myself, but she seems to think talking is bad for me and she spends more time shushing me than actually answering.

What I do learn is this: There are twelve people living in the colony. Thirteen, counting me. Mostly adults, a few teens, one baby who was born here. That part terrifies me to consider. Other than the baby, they were all trapped here one way or another, just like me. They've constructed a life, a community, down here from things they've salvaged and things they've made. The firelight is all that pierces the darkness. They hunt for food, and they hunt for survivors. They do not hunt for a way out.

"Not anymore," says Colleen grimly, when I ask. "It's not worth expending the effort to find something that doesn't exist. You'd do well to accept that, and accept it quickly."

I won't, though. I can't. I haven't seen a lot of the cavern—only a brief glimpse when Colleen helped me to the horrifying outhouse-like situation they've constructed—but I saw enough to know that there are *tons* of tunnels branching off this main cavern. There are tunnels in the ceiling, tunnels off the sides. In a giant cave system like this one, those tunnels don't just lead nowhere. Sure, some of them probably loop back around. But *some* of them definitely go someplace else. Which then goes someplace else. And on and on. Maybe finding an exit won't be easy, but it has to be possible.

"How long before my ribs feel better?" I ask. I hate this already and it's only been a matter of hours.

"It depends how bad the injury is," she says. "Usually six weeks or so before something like this heals, but the pain will diminish much faster if it's bruising than if you've cracked or fractured."

"Has anyone ever died here?" I don't know what makes me ask this. It's so morbid, and it's a *very* blunt question. Immediately, my telltale anxiety symptoms start cropping up. I flex my fingers as though it'll stave off the tingling.

"Well . . . yes." Colleen's equally blunt answer throws me off entirely, which must show on my face, because she's quick to go on: "I'm sorry. It's just—it's inevitable, isn't it? This is a very dangerous place, as you've already seen. Not everyone is so lucky as to end up here where we're safe, where we're protected. Which means, not everyone makes it."

I want to ask whether anyone who's part of the colony has died here, but I can guess the answer and I decide I don't want confirmation.

"You should try to get some sleep," Colleen says, squeezing my hand. "I'll keep checking in on you, and I'll have some food brought to you a little later."

I don't argue because I *am* exhausted. I don't know what time of day it is or what time of day they consider it, but I guess that doesn't matter so much. Alone in the tent, I close my eyes. But I'm not *comfortable* here. Colleen has been kind and welcoming, and that boy killed the monster that tried to kill me. But that doesn't mean the people here are friendly. They could very well be buttering me up so that my guard is down when the time comes for things to turn sinister.

You're being insane, Eliza, I whisper sternly inside my head. It doesn't help. I feel anxious, and not the way I usually feel anxious. *Paranoid* might be more accurate. It makes me trembly and restless.

I do sleep, but it's haunted, fitful. Colleen checks in on me at least once that I'm semi-conscious for. She makes me nervous because she's a stranger, but she's also a comfort because she's a *person* and knowing I won't wander this underground labyrinth alone until I die is more of a relief than I care to admit.

I don't know how much rest I actually get, but when my food arrives, I'm awake, sitting up, and wincing against the pain in my ribs.

The food bringer is a black-haired, pale-skinned teenager who enters the tent with trepidation.

"Hi," she says with a soft smile. "I'm Eleanor."

I try to return the smile, but it's like Sherri always says: I'm not a brave person. Right now, I feel less brave than ever. My smile probably looks more like a snarl. "I'm Eliza."

She sets down a stone-carved bowl filled with something mushy. "Nice to meet you. Everyone is so excited that you're here."

I can't help a slight lift of my eyebrows. "Excited? Really?"

"Well." She bites her lip. "That probably sounds wrong. But the thing is, it's inevitable that people get lost down here, you know? We're always excited when someone joins us alive. It's super preferable to finding them . . . not so alive, later."

"Fair point, I guess."

"In the interest of keeping you alive," she says with a wry smile, "have some dinner!"

I eye the bowl warily. The whitish substance steams. So it's cooked, I guess. Eleanor looks so eager, I try not to seem reluctant when I scoop up a bite with the roughly spoon-shaped piece of stone she handed me.

I chew slowly, trying to figure out what this tastes like. It's meat. I think. The general texture and look reminds me a little of fish. Or crustacean, maybe. The flavor's pretty bland.

It's definitely *not* fish, though. Or crustacean. Or anything I've ever eaten.

I want to know what it is.

But also . . . I don't.

"You're wondering what you're eating, aren't you?"

"Yeah," I admit.

"Insect."

Oh gross. *Gross.* I stop chewing.

"Now, before you knew what it was, did eating it bother you?"

I swallow and the lump of meat settles like a stone. "I guess it didn't. How are there enough bugs down here for all this meat?"

"They're, uh . . . not ordinary insects. They're pretty large. Don't worry, though. They don't come into our cavern; we have to hunt them."

"That . . . isn't really soothing."

She laughs, a surprised sound. She didn't expect me to make a joke. "Yeah," she says. "I guess it's not."

I force down more of the insect, reminding myself that before I knew what it was, I found the taste bland but inoffensive.

"So . . . how long have you been here?" I ask, hoping I'm not being too nosy.

"Two years. I was sixteen."

That information surges like acid in my veins. *I'm* six-teen. I can't fathom losing the next two years of my life to this cave. "Two years," I repeat. "And you've never found a way out?"

"There isn't one," Eleanor says, very definitively. "But you'll stop minding after a while." She smiles, taking my bowl. "I know right now it feels awful. It always does at first. But then you start to love it, eventually."

I am *never* going to love a place that keeps me from my family, from my home. But I don't say that. "It is a very interest-ing cave system," I say instead.

"You been to a lot?"

"As many as I can. I . . . really love rocks and caves and the earth. I am, uh . . . *was* planning to study geology in college."

"Well, Eliza." Eleanor stands, squeezes my arm. "You might do better here than anyone expected."

She leaves and a pit lodges in my stomach. What does she mean by that? Do I look like the type of person who usually does poorly here? I settle into my cot, wincing at the breath-snatching pain in my ribs.

This *cannot* be the place where I die.

I'm kept in isolation for "twenty-four hours." Colleen doesn't use the word *isolation*, but despite the fact that no one has watches or other time-telling devices, they apparently think they can accurately track the passage of time.

"It's a *feeling*," Colleen explains. "Think about it. Early humans didn't have clocks, but their bodies understood when it was time to rest and when it was time to wake up."

I don't argue because arguing stresses me out, but if I *were* to argue, I would point out that early humans had a nice little helper with the telling of time: the sun.

Being an introvert, I don't mind the isolation in theory. I'm getting comfortable enough with Colleen, and I really like Eleanor, who continues to bring me meals. But it worries me that they seem to have a standard isolation period. Why? What are they trying to prevent?

I ask Eleanor, because she's more open than Colleen is.

"Oh, it's . . . people who come here are kind of disoriented sometimes. It's just to give everyone time to adjust. And to see what the new person's going to be like. It's for your benefit, and for ours. Eases the transition. And makes it obvious if a newcomer isn't going to be . . . um . . . suitable." Fear must show on my face. She hurries on. "You're fine! I mean, like, if they're violent or something. If it seems like they might endanger us."

"Oh." My heart beats so hard it hurts. For a moment I was convinced she was using this as a lead-in to tell me I'm not welcome to stay. "That makes sense. You wouldn't want a murderer or something living here."

She smiles. "I mean, it might liven things up sometimes."

"The dangerous things in the caves aren't enough for you?"

"You'll see. After a while, they really lose their fear factor."

She severely underestimates my ability to fear things. If it has teeth and it's willing to bite my face off, I will fear it.

"What happens to the people who don't get to stay?"

"Nothing, really. They just . . . don't stay. It's only happened once since I've lived here."

It's supposed to be soothing, probably, but the idea that the colony turns people out to face the cave's mercy alone unnerves me. What if I do something wrong? Will I be rejected, too?

What feels like a couple hours later, Colleen tells me it's time for me to meet everyone. That they're going to visit me one at a time, which is my personal hell. Meeting new people stresses me out anyway, but meeting people one-on-one is the *worst*. I panic and I get clammed up and I sound like a moron. Which is exactly what happens when the residents of the colony start trickling through. I meet a lot of people whose names blur together, and then I meet Grayson. He's the boy who shot that creature. And he's . . . extremely cute. Sharp-angled face, green eyes, broad smile and shoulders, rumpled brown hair.

He introduces himself to me so politely, handshake and everything. His palm is cool and mine is clammy and he must be feeling pretty repulsed right about now.

"So, um, thanks," I say awkwardly. "For not letting that thing eat me."

He laughs. "It would've been a pretty gross mess to clean up."

"It was probably a pretty gross mess to clean up anyway. Though I guess . . . less scattered pieces or whatever." I hear myself babbling but cannot convince my mouth to close itself. The beginning sensation of panic lodges in my chest. I've met too many people and I haven't yet grasped what is happening to me and why couldn't Grayson have been a forty-year-old man so I don't have this confusing flutter in my stomach? "Anyway," I continue, totally breathless, "I really thought I was going to die and I'm not at all ready to die, so . . ."

"You're welcome," he says, fidgeting like maybe he doesn't know what to do with my appreciation. "And I can't say I'm glad you're here, because that's . . . not a thing to be glad about. But I'm glad you made it. And . . . welcome to the colony, Eliza."

When he leaves, I'm relieved, but I also sort of wish he would have stayed. He was kind and his voice had a softness to it, a soothing quality.

Colleen returns with an understanding smile.

"Was that everyone?" I ask, trying not to sound too eager for the introductions to be over. I wasn't keeping close track of the numbers but I must be close, at least.

"Just about," says Colleen. "For now, yes, it's everyone. You're starting to look a little tired, and I think—"

She breaks off mid-sentence when a man barges into the tent.

"Glenn," she says in a warning tone, but he pushes past her anyway.

"Welcome," he says. I think it's supposed to be friendly, but his tone is cold.

"Thank you."

"You arrived here with a backpack?"

"Um, yes?"

"Excellent, what did you bring?"

My backpack sits next to me on the bed, and I clutch it to my side. Glenn seems to realize then that he's frightening me. His severe expression softens. "I'm sorry," he says. "It's just that we share supplies here. So if you had anything that would be useful to the group . . ."

"Oh." I bite my lip. Sharing seems like the right thing to do, but at the same time, I'm reluctant to give up any of my stuff. "Well, I lost my headlamp, but—"

"Already found it." Glenn smiles.

"Oh. Um. Okay. Well, I have another flashlight." I unzip my backpack and pull it out.

Glenn takes it, peering inside the pack. "Is that a first-aid kit? A pocketknife? You came prepared."

I hand them both over, and my jacket, spare outfit, batteries, snacks, and water bottle, too. He lets me keep my phone. Then we get to my journal.

"Oh, paper!" he exclaims. "Excellent, a rare commodity."

"I can't—I'm not giving you this, I'm sorry."

"But—"

"Glenn." Colleen intercedes with a hand gripping his forearm. "This girl needs to rest; she has bruised ribs. And you've just ransacked her things. This is not the right way to greet new residents."

Their eyes are both storms as they stare at each other for a painfully long time.

"You're right," Glenn says finally, and turns to me. "I'm very sorry, Eliza, I get a little intense about things. Keep the journal."

"Thank you," I whisper, but he's already out of the tent.

The first time I met Meg, she was crying. It was fourth grade and Toby Millerson had just stolen her dessert, or so she claimed. I never checked to see if it was true. I just put an arm around her and offered her mine.

"No," she said between sniffles. "Yours looks really good but mine was made special by my mom. If I can't have that, I don't even want anything."

She liked being comforted, though. And Meg required comforting on a pretty regular basis from then on. I never minded, usually. It came naturally to me. It didn't make me anxious.

It got to be a lot sometimes, though. The emotional weight of caring for her as well as myself. It was just so constant. But Meg was my friend. She texted me all the time; she made me feel seen.

Somehow, that never felt worth giving up on.

7

The next morning, I'm finally freed from my tent-prison. Semi-healed. Like a butterfly fresh from the cocoon, when its wings are still all limp and useless, but at least it's out in the world. Colleen leads me, which I'm thankful for. My heart hums so fast it feels like it's skipping beats. My palms could water a garden.

Everyone was kind when I met them last night, but it's different outside the tent. I don't know how to insert myself into an already-formed group like this. I barely know how to insert myself into my own friendships. And I'm still wrapping my mind around the part where I'm trapped underground.

Possibly forever.

Probably forever.

A lot of tunnels lead off this room. Some of them are high up, like the one I tumbled out of—a few with makeshift ladders dangling from their openings—and some are at floor level. One is actually *in* the floor, near the middle of the room, and it feels like a death trap. They keep it covered over so no one falls in. I'm told that through one of the side tunnels is another room with a river carved through it and a waterfall dropping into the abyss below. This room is dry, other than just enough condensation to leave surfaces slick. Hides have been placed over much of the floor, which lessens the danger of walking. They're from creatures like the thing that chased me, Colleen explained when I asked. Stitched together, these same hides are what cover the tents that line the cave's walls. The residents have removed most of the cave formations and smoothed over the ground beneath, but the ceiling's high enough that some stalactites and draperies dangle untouched. A single, small fire glows at the center of the room, and I'm curious how they keep it lit.

"Welcome back to life," a voice says from behind me.

I turn, and there stands Eleanor, hair draped over her shoulder in a loose braid. "Now that you're out and about, you should come hang out with us!"

"Us?"

"Yeah." She smiles again. "We youths need to stick together. Come on!"

I glance up at Colleen, who nods encouragingly.

"Okay. Where are we going?"

"To the river."

She says this the same way you'd say it aboveground. Like it's a hot day and we're just gonna go for a swim. Totally normal. And she hooks her arm through mine as though we're already friends. It makes my stomach feel like a swarm of bees. What if these people think I'm weird? What if I end up ostracized in this tiny community? Where would I even go from here?

It's not that I'm planning to live in the colony forever. I want to go home. I *have* to. But I also have to face the reality that all these people would not have stayed in this cave with its darkness and moist walls and semi-putrid stale smell if they could leave.

Eleanor leads me through a short but pitch-black tunnel into another cavern. This one is *loud*, thanks to the thunderous crashing of a waterfall at one side. A fire flickers halfway between where I stand and the edge of the river that cuts through the room. It's an even smaller fire than in the main cavern, but lights well enough that I can see all the way to the far side, though much of it is cloaked in shadow. Driftwood's piled up near the fire. Drying, I realize.

Like in the other room, all the cave formations on this side of the river have been cleared away, leaving semi-flat ground. But a makeshift bridge crosses the river where it's at its narrow-est, and on the far side, they left everything untouched.

A couple people hang out near the bank just to the left of the bridge, away from the waterfall. I sweep my eyes past them, following the river to where a low-ceilinged opening spits it out.

"You have to meet the others," Eleanor says, tugging gently on my arm. "I mean, meet them in a more real way."

My insides roil again, but I *do* want to hang out with the other people my age, so I take as deep a breath as my healing-but-still-achy ribs allow and follow her. "This is Alice and Grayson, in case you didn't remember their names."

"I actually did remember, but I'm terrible with names, so that's pretty much a miracle, to be honest."

They all smile, and the knot inside me loosens a tiny bit. Maybe I'll do okay after all. If this small group will welcome me, the larger population will be less terrifying.

Eleanor sits at the edge of the river, rolling up her pant legs. I mimic her, grimacing at the flare of pain in my ribs as I bend, and dip my toes in. The water's warmer than I expected. Not as warm as the lake I swam through before, but not too chilly, either.

Alice is on the other side of Eleanor. She's extremely pretty. The kind of pretty that makes my nausea start up again. She's dark-skinned with long, dense curls. Faded color in the tips tells me that it was once dyed red. Not orange-red, like my hair, but red-red, like the feathers of a cardinal. Her eyes are deep brown, her lashes and nose are long, and she has dimples in her cheeks and chin.

Grayson, who paces the water's edge, I cannot look at, because I'm still dying of embarrassment at how he saved my life and how awkward I was when we met.

"How are your ribs feeling?" Alice asks. All of them are watching me. But, I guess, what did I expect?

My throat is a desert and my voice cracks when I say, "Pretty sore. Getting better, though."

Alice catches a mangled tree branch that's floating by and sets it down close to Grayson.

"Careful with that thing!" He flinches away. "I'd like to keep both my eyes, thanks."

"Where does that river come from?" I blurt out, while Alice is busy laughing.

"We can't get out that way, if that's what you're asking," Grayson says in a sorrow-tinged voice. He sits down next to Alice.

I shrug like that's not why I was asking, but it hits hard to hear him say it.

"The ceiling gets too low," Alice elaborates. "Nowhere to come up for air. So you'd drown."

So we really are trapped. I want to say it, but it's too depressing and I don't want to be the girl who comes in and sucks the joy out of everybody. Not when they're still watching me curiously, and I know they'll discuss what they think of me next time we're apart.

I notice a woman examining some of the structures on the far side of the cavern. She appears to be taking measurements on a stalagmite.

"Who's that?" I ask Eleanor. "I didn't meet her."

Her eyes follow my gaze. "Oh, that's Mary. She's our nerd."

She says *nerd* without cruelty, but my stomach clenches.

No one will ever date you if you don't stop being such a nerd. Cut it out with the nerd stuff; nobody wants to listen to that crap. You are such a nerd, Eliza; you're lucky we hang out with you.

Stop, I command my brain. *Stop it right now.*

"She's a scientist," Eleanor elaborates. "Like a geologist or something. She's . . . a little odd, but she knows *everything.*"

My stomach clenches again, but in a different way, now. A

hopeful way. Eleanor speaks of Mary so reverently. Like her knowledge, her *nerdiness*, is impressive. Worthy of respect.

"I want to be a geologist when I grow up," I blurt out, and then feel myself blush.

Grayson looks straight at me and I think I might literally die.

"Really?" Alice sounds interested.

"Yeah, I mean . . . I like rocks and the earth and stuff."

"Huh." Alice frowns thoughtfully. "That's ambitious. I don't even know what I want—would have wanted to be."

Grayson chews on the inside of his lip for a long moment, and then says, "Maybe together, you and Mary can find us a way out of here."

Alice elbows him in the ribs. "Would you *stop* with that? You know how pointless it is."

He shrugs, frowns, and looks away. Then mutters, "Nothing's pointless except giving up."

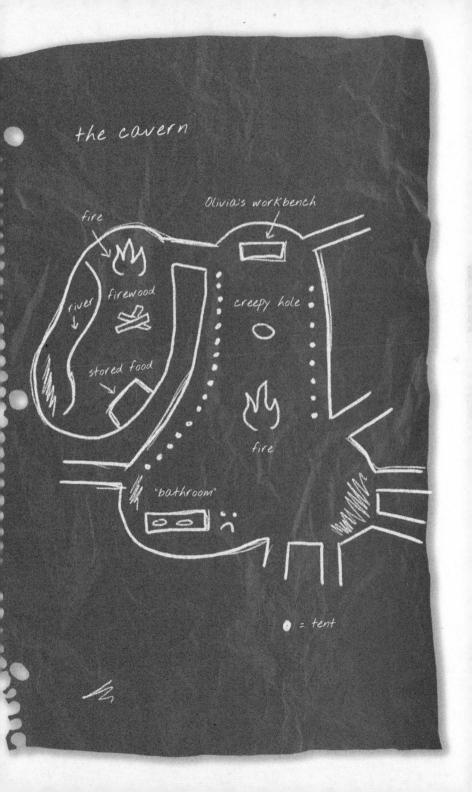

8

I meet Mary later in the day, pretty much by accident. Eleanor explained to me privately that the reason Mary didn't come meet me when all the others did is because she's a bit odd. "Not because of the geology thing," she was quick to add. "She's just sort of . . . She can be hard to interact with. *Very* brilliant, though."

My ribs are doing better—confirming that they are bruised and not broken—but breathing and too much activity still hurts, so Colleen told me not to overdo my participation just yet. I'm listening to her but also I don't want to sit around awkwardly while everyone else chips in to help keep this place running. So during working hours I follow Eleanor around, which actually helps me get a feel of the routine.

But when I leave her side to pay the outhouse a visit, I notice something that sidetracks me. Against the far wall of the cavern sits a table that's made from a flowstone formation with its top scraped flat. It's covered in an array of rock and mineral samples, plus some cave formations that have been cut away from their original locations.

Curious, I pick up one of the mineral formations, inspecting it. With the poor lighting, I have to bring it pretty close to my face to take a guess at what the almost turquoise-looking specimen is.

"Malachite," says a voice behind me.

I whirl around, formation still clutched in my fist. It's Mary, standing behind me, expressionless. "Is it? That was going to be my guess. I've never seen it raw before."

She looks startled.

"Hmm, interesting." She holds out a palm, on which I set the chunk of malachite. "So you actually know some things."

"I—well, I'm sixteen, so I have been in school for a while."

"I mean about geology."

"Oh. Yeah. It's what I want to major in when I go to college."

"Excellent." She beams at me. I return her smile, observing her in a way I hope is subtle. Mary's in her thirties, if I had to guess, with long blond hair tied neatly into a ponytail. She's slender—well, *gaunt* is probably more accurate; everyone here has a bit of a wasted look. And she's a *very* intense person.

Immediately, she starts quizzing me on all sorts of things. Types of rocks she's got sitting out. The names of different styles of cave formations. The layers of the earth. She even gives me math problems. I am, fortunately, pretty excellent at math, and I can tell Mary's glad about it. I'm getting a little stressed; it's like taking the PSATs with no warning and hoping everything turns out okay. And after the math problems, it gets weirder.

Mary starts asking me about my thoughts since I've been down here, digging really deep about my anxiety and what it is usually versus what it is right now. How I feel about this cave. What my family life was like and if I want to go home. I'm honest with her about everything, which terrifies me, but I feel, somehow, like she'll be able to tell if I lie.

She whips out a battered spiral notebook and starts scribbling furiously in it.

"You have a journal, too?" I resist the urge to peer over the top of it for a glimpse of what she's writing. I wonder if she, too, had to fight with Glenn in order to keep this.

Her pen halts its movement. "*You* have one?"

"Yeah. I mean, there's not a lot in it right now. My friends and I were planning to go to this cave up on the mountain and . . ." I hesitate, worried that I'm boring her, but she doesn't *seem* bored. "Anyway, I wanted to bring a notebook in case I saw anything interesting. I guess . . . I *have* seen some interesting stuff."

She barks a laugh. "I guess so." She leans closer to me, radiating intensity. "Don't stop writing in that journal, okay? Even if you start to feel . . . I don't know, *comfortable* here, keep writing things down. And keep reading what you've written. You *do* want to go home, you said?"

She says all of this so fast that it takes several seconds before I realize she's stopped. "Of course! More than anything."

"Good. *Do not* forget that." A haunted expression crosses her face, and when she speaks again, her voice is low and shaken. "You *cannot* let yourself forget."

"I won't." I cross my arms tight, like I can press the bad feeling out of my chest. "Why would I forget? I need to—my family thinks I'm dead. They have to know that I'm not and that I love them and I miss them."

A thick lump knots in my throat. I can't swallow it away.

"Have you always kept a journal?" Mary asks.

I nod.

"Have you ever read back through entries from when you were younger and seen how *passionate* you were about something, but in retrospect, you couldn't recall that feeling, or even begin to understand it anymore?"

"I guess." My voice comes out hoarse. Every time I think of my family, it practically knocks the wind out of me.

"Read back through the things you write in that journal," she says, holding hers tight in both fists. "Read it every day and remember what is in there. Even if you stop being able to understand how you felt about certain things, think about it logically. Know that you *did* feel that way, and that there was a reason, and don't let yourself become complacent."

"Okay," I whisper.

She frowns and sets down her notebook. "I'm sorry. I'm scaring you. I'm just—this is a geologist's dream, Eliza." She spreads her arms wide. "It's got *everything*. But it's so easy to be taken in by the beauty, by the power of it all. You have to be— you have to stay really strong. Keep your mind clear. Not let the whispers of the cave speak to you too strongly."

I don't understand what she means and I wish she wouldn't

be so cryptic, but I'm afraid of what she might say if I ask her to be more blunt.

There is something about this place that creeps inside of you. This bad-smelling cavern with its shadowed corners and uncomfortable beds and terrifying creatures already feels a little bit like home to me, after barely any time. But I would never want to live here more than I wanted to live in my *actual* home. That's an absurd thought.

Isn't it?

"There you are!" Eleanor approaches, jovial and unscary. "I was getting bored without you."

I grin and hope it isn't too dorky. It's a little embarrassing how long it's been since someone outside my family made me feel like my presence was wanted rather than put up with. "Sorry."

She waves away my apology. "You say sorry too much. Anyway, Mary, just FYI, Glenn thinks he saw a bioluminescent, so he said we should all be on the alert for the time being."

"What does that mean?" I ask nervously. "What's a bioluminescent?"

"They're *nothing*," says Mary, annoyed.

Eleanor's eyes glint and she leans closer to me. "If you go deeper, you'll find these other people-like creatures who were born down here. And they *don't* like us." Her tone is casual but her words are straight out of a horror movie.

Goose bumps prick my skin from toes to scalp.

"Goodness, Eleanor, you do have a flair for the dramatic." Mary puts down the rock she was holding. "We don't know where they live, Eliza. Or how many there are. They don't seem to like venturing up this way, but we've come across them before with hunting parties, and from time to time, we think we spot one."

"Are they like . . . regular people who happen to live underground?" Of course they're not. Or else Eleanor wouldn't have called them *people-like creatures* or *bioluminescents*. This creeps the heck out of me. I never should have let Sherri talk me into watching *The Descent*.

"Sort of. But also . . . no." Mary picks up a mineral formation and begins inspecting it. "We call them the bioluminescents because, well . . . they are. They glow."

"And they don't speak our language," Eleanor adds.

"If they did, I'd be deeply concerned about who taught them," Mary says.

And then I remember—the glowing *thing* I saw. It was a person, one of these bioluminescent beings. "I think—I think I saw one," I say.

"Really?" Mary sets down the formation. "When?"

I describe what I saw, and they're both riveted. "Have either of you seen one?" I ask.

Eleanor shakes her head. "Only the skeleton."

Mary doesn't answer.

"What would happen if they . . . tried to attack us?"

Mary sighs. "We don't actually know that they're hostile; everyone just assumes."

"Oh come on." Eleanor folds her arms tight. "They attacked Glenn two months ago. We *know* they're hostile."

Mary opens her mouth to respond, but that's when a sound almost like a clanging bell alerts everyone that it's time for dinner. It sounds before every meal, and it scared the crap out of me every time when I was isolated in my tent.

"I guess we'll pick this discussion back up later," Mary says tightly.

"I guess we will." Eleanor scowls.

The tension between them bothers me. I feel like it's my fault for asking about the other humans, but I don't want to apologize, because Eleanor said I do it too much. So I say nothing.

Dinner is everyone sitting on the cave floor around the fire and eating food from stone-carved bowls. From what I understand of the system, everyone takes turns cooking the meals, but it's nothing fancy for obvious reasons. I guess eventually I'll help cook, too. Earlier, I watched Eleanor disembowel a dead and very large insect, and I can't say it wasn't interesting. But I can't say it made the prospect of eating insect forever any more appealing, either.

Eleanor and I sit with Grayson and Alice. The three of them immediately strike up an easy conversation, totally carefree. I stomp on the part of me that's jealous. Among the three, Grayson arrived most recently, a few months ago. Alice has been here over a year, and Eleanor nearly two. Of *course* they've bonded. It doesn't mean I'll never be part of the group. But my brain is a troll and it tells me they're already settled, that they might not want me, and that I have no other options.

I try to keep up with their conversation as I eat, but Alice and Eleanor are gossiping about some of the adults, and I don't remember everyone's names yet, so I'm basically lost, even as Eleanor tries to include me, subtly pointing out the people relevant to the discussion.

By the time the meal is over, I'm starting to feel very stressed, a little sweaty, and like I might devolve into a panic attack soon. I excuse myself with a weak story about needing something from my tent, and hide myself behind its closed flaps.

It's easier to breathe in the tent. Doesn't feel like the world's collapsing on top of me, like my lungs are being vacuum-sealed. This colony is a nightmare for the socially anxious. We're here to survive, and survival is a team effort. No one's asking me to do much of anything yet, but the group has to work together in order to keep this thing going. There aren't enough of us for anyone to sit around, not pulling their weight. My tent is dark; it's quiet. I've always felt better in the dark. It's like a warm blanket closing me off from the gazes of people who make me uncomfortable.

I don't know how long I've been sitting alone when there's a gentle knock on the pole at the front of my tent.

"Uh, come in?"

The flap lifts, and here's Grayson, holding out a cup. "I thought you might like some water or something."

I don't want to send him away because that's incredibly rude, but alone time with a cute guy is basically the least helpful thing that could happen to me right now.

"Thank you." I take the cup. I *am* thirsty.

He lingers, and the awkwardness is practically sentient.

"You know," he says, sitting tentatively on the opposite side of my cot, "there's nothing wrong with not being just . . . instantly okay with everything. This place *sucks*. I mean, it's better than nothing, but it's not . . . no one *wants* this."

I take a gulp of my water, thinking.

Apparently not thinking fast enough, because he goes on: "I mean, we have to hunt for food *every day*. We can't store anything very long; it spoils. We rely on fire for food and light, and if we ever run out of driftwood, we're screwed. We don't have normal building materials or food or—"

"This is not . . ." I'm partway through my sentence before I realize I've interrupted, and the realization horrifies me. The rest of my sentence is more like a whisper. ". . . not helping me panic less."

He shuts up altogether, the muscles in his throat rippling like he's literally swallowing his words.

"I shouldn't have said that," I rush on. "It's just—you're right. This isn't a situation a person can be okay with right away, and I'm not. Honestly, I think I'm still in shock. Like, how can this *possibly* be something that happened in real life? I don't know how to live in this reality. I can't adjust. I'm not usually so rude, and I don't usually ramble like this, I'm . . ."

"I get it." He smiles sadly. "This is the best home we could ask for down here, but even still, I've been here five months and I don't know how to live in this reality. I don't think I ever will."

"What happened?" I ask. "To make you end up here, I mean."

"Poor life choices," he says dryly. "I was exploring an abandoned mine shaft just outside my town. It's all blocked off and has a million warning signs about its instability, but people go in there all the time to drink and stuff. I got brave or stupid or both, I guess, and decided I should explore a little deeper. Figured out the warnings about instability weren't for nothing when I fell through a weak spot and ended up in this weird, narrow corridor of rock. Three days of wandering later, I saw firelight, and dropped from above. I'm lucky I lived, honestly."

"Where are you from?" I ask. The only person whose hometown I've asked about so far is Colleen. She lived in Albany, which is about a twenty-minute drive from my town.

"Near Cobleskill," he says.

Not too far from me, then. But in the opposite direction of Albany. I wish it helped me figure out where we are. All it does is make me believe this cave system is truly massive. How much of the state does it stretch across?

"And how'd *you* end up down here?" he asks.

"I was near a swamp and got swallowed up by a sinkhole. It spit me out in an underground cavern, and then I was wandering around for a while before I started getting chased by that thing and then . . . well, you know the rest." I feel shy again, reminding him of my dramatic entrance. "How did you learn to shoot arrows like that, anyway?"

"I go bow hunting every year. So . . . a lot of practice."

"Does everyone here have some kind of survival skills?"

He laughs. "Definitely not. Most of what you'd learn up above doesn't help too much down here."

"You mean you *didn't* take How to Survive When Trapped in a Deep Underground Cave System 101 in school?"

He laughs again. Something unwinds inside me. We're chatting and he's laughing and it's going fine. I will get through this.

"You know what's funny, in, like, a very gallows humor way?" I say, because now that I'm socializing like a normal person, it's almost a high, and I feel emboldened. "The swamp I went into, it's called Drowners Swamp. People have gone missing there before, and we actually have a myth that it's because the sinkholes lead to a passage to the center of the earth. Which is so crazy, but . . ."

"But also not that crazy," Grayson finishes for me.

It dawns on me now that if people have gone missing in that swamp, if they really were swallowed up by sinkholes like me and none of them are here, then either they suffocated at the muddy bottom when the sinkholes filled back in, or they made it to the cavern system but didn't find this place. Putting things in that perspective, I'm pretty lucky.

Another thing to consider: If the myth exists, that could mean someone really came here and made it out, couldn't it?

"You should talk to Mary about the center-of-the-earth thing," Grayson says. He fidgets with a hole in his jeans. "Because based on her research, we're deeper than should be possible to withstand for both temperature and pressure, and she thinks we're in some sort of anomaly, that we could keep going, all the way through the earth's crust to the next layer."

"That's totally insane."

He shrugs. "Don't ask me, I'm not a scientist. But she's explained it before, and it makes sense. You're into this geology stuff, right? You'll probably understand it way more."

Okay, I know it's not *that* big a deal he remembered I'm into geology, because it's one of, like, four things he knows about me, but my insides dance anyway.

"I guess I'll have to ask her about it. Not like I don't have plenty of time, right?" I attempt a smile but it falls flat.

My future used to be wide open. There are so many schools in this country where I can study geology. So many *good* schools. And after that, infinite career options. No matter how much Sherri and Meg teased me about being a nerd, I was hopeful about that. I knew eventually, there'd be other people like me and things wouldn't be so hard. Now, suddenly, the only thing in front of me is unending blackness. And it's not even meta-phorical blackness. If I leave this cavern, it will inhale me.

I'm trapped, and the bleakness is so all-consuming, I can't even think about it.

This community was started nine years ago. Its first resident was completely alone down here but had found evidence of an old camp. Colleen told me that, when I was still lying here help-lessly in bed. But when I asked who the founder was, she deftly changed the subject in a way that made me suspect an unpleas-ant death. Seems like a lot of people who've lived here have died.

I can't imagine being here for nine years. I can't imagine being here for nine *weeks*.

"How do you . . . keep going?" I ask in a soft, hesitant voice.

Grayson hangs his head and a silence yawns between us for several seconds before he answers. "It's different for everyone. But the only way I've found is to believe with my whole entire heart that, eventually, something will change. That this isn't forever. Because if this is forever . . ."

He doesn't finish the sentence. And I don't try to make him.

The first time I met Sherri, she was laughing. Boisterously. Throwing back her head and flashing her teeth in front of a circle of boys. There was this thing Sherri's always been good at, and it's convincing boys she'll do anything, even though it's a total lie. She mesmerizes them with her laugh. Teases them with her hints and her innuendos, but never actually follows through on anything she implies she'll do.

I admire a lot of things about Sherri, though. The easy way she talks to people. How she can get a group to surround her, the natural ease with which she leads people. She knows what she wants and she believes that the things she wants will happen, which means they usually do. It's an abrasive trait but also an admirable one.

It's the reason I always followed her.

9

"How are your ribs feeling?" Colleen asks the next morning. Or, what they're calling morning. I'm keeping track of time with a mark in my journal every time I wake up.

I press a hand to my side. "Okay. Less sore than yesterday."

"Good. Because you need to start learning our routine." She smiles warmly. "You can follow me around for a little bit, and I'll show you—"

"I need an intern," Mary interrupts.

Colleen rolls not only her eyes but her entire head in Mary's direction. "This isn't a college campus. You don't need an intern as much as the rest of us need to eat."

"Oh really?" Mary folds her arms, nostrils flaring. "My work hasn't helped us out with that at all?"

"Of course it has, or you wouldn't still be doing it."

"Oh *really*?"

Colleen sighs. "That's not even the point, Mary. Eliza is healing and she needs to start learning how to be part of our community. You know how it works."

Mary stands firm, her sharp-angled chin jutted forward. "Eliza's scientifically minded. She can do the menial stuff sometimes, but other times, I need her to—"

"The *menial* stuff?" Colleen's eyes could shoot lasers.

Watching these two adult women fight—about me?—turns the stress fractures in my brain into stress ravines. Especially as Mary clearly lacks any amount of tact whatsoever and I can see this thing escalating real fast.

"That sounds like a compromise," Eleanor interrupts, actually inserting herself physically between the two women. Eleanor's tall, taller than either of them. "Not everyone has to help our community in the exact same way. Eliza can do more than one thing."

"Glenn isn't going to like this," says Colleen.

"Screw Glenn," says Mary.

I just stay where I am, sitting uselessly, fingertips prickling with anxiety. Eleanor doesn't seem to know what else to say, either.

"You can have her for a little while in the mornings," Colleen says, glancing down at me with a slight frown. I feel like I've disappointed her somehow, even though all I did was exist.

"Works for now." Mary looks down at me, too, only her expression is more victorious.

And just like that, I belong to Mary.

She doesn't give me a moment to catch my breath, either. She steers me at once to her workstation, and the grilling she gave me yesterday about everything I've ever learned continues. My head aches like it does after a particularly grueling test. And then she gets down to the point.

"Did you reread your journal last night like I told you to?"

"Yes," I say, even though it's a lie. I've been keeping the journal for, like, three days. Everything in it is still very fresh.

"Good. And you still feel like you want to go home?"

"Of course." But I get a weird feeling in my stomach when I say that. I *do*, of course, but something deep within me whispers, *No, you don't*. The second I get back to my tent this evening, I'm rereading that journal.

Mary leans toward me, brow furrowed. "What's making your face look like that?"

I startle. "That's what my face looks like."

"No, your expression. When you answered my question, it changed."

"Oh, um, I don't know. I had a feeling like I was lying even though I wasn't."

She rakes her fingers through her hair, loosening her ponytail messily. "I knew it. I knew you didn't have long."

"Long before *what*?"

She frowns. "Have you ever heard of nitrogen narcosis?"

"It happens to divers, right? When they go too deep and they start to feel kind of drunk and, like, hallucinate and stuff?"

"Exactly." She seems pleased that I knew the answer, but there's something wild about her still. "I have a theory that we're experiencing something similar here. Not the *same*, or we'd all be acting erratically, there wouldn't be a pattern. But something in the air down here, it makes us odd. It makes us believe we are happy here, but it also makes us anxious, paranoid."

"Have you told the others this?"

She laughs dryly. "Did I mention paranoid? People don't want to believe their minds aren't under their control."

"That's why you told me to keep rereading my journal. So I'll remember."

She nods. "It sets in pretty fast. But you're the best chance we've had in quite some time, Eliza. Our best chance to escape."

"But how?" It's a lot of pressure. An overwhelming amount. "Even if I somehow don't get trapped mentally, aren't we still trapped physically?"

"Maybe." Mary's cagey all of a sudden. "Or maybe we just haven't looked in the right direction."

She glances at the covered tunnel in the floor.

"Deeper?" I ask, eyebrows raised.

She shrugs. "Worked for Jules Verne, didn't it?"

Yeah, in fiction. "Has anyone tried going down that tunnel?"

"Oh, you can't. There was a cave-in a while back, before I came. That's why no one's allowed down anymore."

Now that she mentions it, I remember Colleen telling me that, on my first day. To stay away from that tunnel; it wasn't safe. There's something to what Mary's saying right now that makes sense to me, though. That makes me want to go deeper into this cave and see what happens.

As though reading my mind, Mary says quietly, "You barely know me, Eliza, and I'm sure you don't particularly trust me, but please hear this. If you want to leave here, there isn't much time to figure things out. It will be difficult and it will be dangerous. But people who stay, they don't last. We're all going to die down here eventually, inevitably. It feels safe in our little cavern, but it isn't. It doesn't take long before leaving is the last thing on your mind. And the only thing you'll have as a reminder that you once wanted to go will be your journal."

"*You* have a journal, and you obviously know that you once wanted to leave." I fold my arms tight across my chest, holding in a heart that feels like it's trying to flee. "Why don't you go?"

Mary's entire body shudders. "I . . . Things are different for me. I can't explain it. I want to say 'you'll understand,' but the whole reason I've told you all of this is because I hope you never get to that point. There are people who would leave, if someone led. I promise you that."

I glance at the hide-covered tunnel again. I don't like the implication in her words. That I have to somehow be a leader, be a hero. Everything I've done to get here in the first place makes me feel like such a follower. What was I thinking? I've always been so completely my own person. Meg didn't always like it, but she understood it. Yet ever since Sherri came into our lives, everything's changed. I've felt them both leaving me behind and

I've been desperate not to let them. I haven't been *me*—and even when I *was*, I've never been a leader. I don't have the charisma to get others lining up behind me. I can barely *talk* to people.

But I feel the urgency in Mary's words. The desperation.

And I might be starting to feel a little desperate, too.

Colony daily routine:

* Wake up. Figure out if it seems like other people are moving around, or if it's still night.

* Get dressed and come out of my tent.

* Breakfast. (I'll help cook each meal approx. once a week.)

* Morning activities—I "intern" for Mary, some people go hunting or scavenging, others clean.

* Clean the cavern. It's always dirty. Total lost cause. Something to do, though.

* Lunch, when the hunters return (or when people are hungry if they take too long).

* Help gutting the insects. Apparently I'll do this approx. 4x per week.

* Hang out with everyone OR have alone time OR help Mary with stuff.

* Dinner.

* Clean up dinner.

* Hang out till people start going to bed.

10

After my morning working with Mary, she gives me "lessons" in what she calls sign language. She says there may come a time when we need to speak without words, and she's tried to convince the others of this but none of them have maintained interest. To be honest, I get why. I'm no expert, but I'm positive that this is a language she made up. And I'm not convinced that it'll ever come in handy within the dark bowels of this cave system.

I've got a low-grade headache by the end just from the sheer volume of mental activity I've already engaged in this morning.

Lunch is sitting with Eleanor and Alice—half the colony went "scavenging" this morning and they're not back yet, so no Grayson.

"Colleen wants you to shadow me after lunch," Eleanor says. "She said it seems like a good idea to keep you on the same tasks I'm doing for now since we've bonded."

I slide right by that thing about our bonding because it makes me embarrassingly pleased. "I promise not to slow you down."

She laughs and hooks her arm in mine. "I guarantee you'll be just fine. Most of our day-to-day tasks aren't so difficult, just time-consuming. First up this afternoon, moving dry wood in here from the river cave."

The wood thing is a never-ending cycle.

There's almost always someone in the river cave, keeping an eye out for stray driftwood. We wouldn't die without it. Probably. But the purity of darkness within the cavern would cause madness, after a while. And, eventually, blindness, if we lasted long enough.

"Is there a plan for if we run out of wood?" I ask.

"Not really." Eleanor gathers an armful. "We've never run out of wood, though. We get it here and we find it sometimes and we keep our fires small. We also use animal fat. In the fires and in our torches. I don't know. It's worked so far, and we kinda don't have another option."

I don't press further on the topic because she clearly doesn't have answers for me, and I'm starting to feel annoying. Instead, I mirror her as she carries dried driftwood from the river cavern to the main cavern, dropping it in a messy pile in front of the neatly stacked supply that's already in here. After that, we break the wood into tidier pieces, using a hatchet crafted from stone.

"We used to have a real hatchet," Eleanor says. "But it broke last year."

I hack at a piece of driftwood with the ax. It splits neatly. "This one seems to do the job pretty well."

Eleanor smiles. "It does indeed."

We work in silence for a few minutes. I want to bring up the concept of leaving here, but I'm too chicken. The words form in my head—*If I left, would you come with me?*—but they won't form on my tongue.

"I made it, you know," Eleanor says. "The hatchet."

"Really?" I look at it anew. It's rutted, primitive-looking, but the edge is sharp and the whole thing is solid and easy to grip. Never in a million years would I have the patience to make something like this. "Where did you learn to do that?"

"Oh, my dad was so into how people made tools back in the day. I've been to a million exhibits and whatnot. More than any human should go to." She blinks several times. "I always thought it was a ridiculous thing to be so interested in, but I guess not, huh?"

"Was it just you and your dad?" I ask.

"Yeah. Most of the time. I mean, he had a couple girlfriends over the years but none that stuck. My mom left when I was three. I don't really remember her."

"That's terrible."

She shrugs. "I mean, yeah, it's a pretty crappy thing to do, but my dad and I had a really good life without her. If she didn't want to be with us, I'm glad she didn't stay."

"I guess that's true." This is my opportunity. She clearly misses her dad, loves him a lot. Now is when I should ask her. *If I were to leave, would you leave, too?* It's right there, lodged in my throat like a pill swallowed wrong. Why can't I say it? So what if she tells me no?

"You must miss your dad a lot" is what comes out when I finally do say something. Well, it's better than nothing.

"I do." She snaps a piece of driftwood crisply in half. "He was a really great dad."

The courage finally finds me. "You could still—"

And, of course, I'm interrupted. The scavenging party has returned. They drop down from one of the upper tunnels, which has a rope ladder attached.

"Oh excellent." Eleanor hops up. "Come on! Let's see if they found anything good. Or, you know, anything at all."

Scavenging, apparently, is a weekly activity. Anyone who wants to come along can join, and the group scours the upper tunnels and caverns for anything useful. When Colleen explained this to me, I asked her why they don't also look for a way out.

She didn't even answer.

We all gather around the returned scavengers, who are headed up by Glenn. He's loving the attention, clearly. He seems to thrive on being the focal point of the colony, on being a hunter and a gatherer, on being needed. He's unreasonably intense, though, and he creeps me out.

"It was a good trip," Glenn announces with a wide grin. He sets down a backpack—*my* backpack, I realize with a possessive jolt—that he's filled with items. He takes them out one by one and everyone oohs and aahs like we're watching a fireworks display.

A (dead) flashlight.

Shirt, shorts, and (ew) underwear.

A packet of matches.

Hiking boots.

A book.

A bottle of water, mostly empty.

A chocolate bar.

As everyone descends for a closer look and a bite of the chocolate bar, I swerve, fake-casually, off to the side, where Grayson stands.

"Have fun?" I ask, ignoring the claws in my stomach and the fizz in my fingertips.

"It's always fun." He shoves his hands into his pockets. "You didn't want any of the chocolate?"

"I ate chocolate, like, a week ago. I'd rather let everyone else enjoy it. You?"

"Can't. I am a true loser: allergic to cocoa."

"Wow. I can't really think of a worse allergy."

He laughs. "At least it's easy enough to avoid. Not like gluten or dairy or nuts or something."

"True." I pause. "Where did you find that stuff, anyway?"

"It was, um . . . a person who didn't make it."

That's . . . unpleasantly dark.

"I know it's awful to think about," he goes on hurriedly. "I found it awful at first, and I still do, if I think about it too much. But not everyone makes it, and if they have stuff we can use . . .

We leave them with dignity. We prop them up into a sitting position; it's kind of like our own funeral rites."

"Dignity?" I keep my voice quiet, but the pitch is octaves higher than normal. "Grayson, you take their clothes; you take their *underwear.* You don't leave them with dignity, you—" I cut myself off, thinking of those two skeletons I found. Bare to the bone. "Do you take their *flesh?*"

"God, Eliza, *no.*" He looks utterly horrified. "We haven't stooped to cannibalism, thanks."

"Sorry." I run my hands roughly through my hair. "I'm sorry, I just—came across a couple of your corpses on my way here, and they were pretty much picked to the bone."

"Yeah." He frowns. "Things decompose pretty fast here. And sometimes . . . other stuff eats what we don't."

I shudder, not wanting to think about that at all. We both fidget uncomfortably for a moment. Grayson, luckily, is better at this than I am. "How're your ribs feeling?" he asks.

"Oh." I press a hand lightly to my side. "Not bad. I can breathe now without feeling like my lung is collapsing, so that's a plus."

"Well, if you're feeling so much better," he says, "then you should come with us tomorrow when we go hunting."

"Oh, I don't think so." Inside, I'm laughing hysterically at the very thought, but outside, I hold it together.

"Come on," he insists, facing me, staring at me intently with his lovely green eyes. I feel a little bit faint. "It feels really good to get out of the colony sometimes. I *know* you're feeling stir-crazy here. Plus, you love caves, right? Don't you wanna explore?"

"I don't know," I hedge. "I'll think about it."

"Good," he says. "I would really love it if you come."

When he puts it that way, how can I possibly say no?

I didn't realize that the anxiety I get in social situations wasn't normal until my mom noticed, back in seventh grade, when I had a full-blown panic attack about going to a school dance. A therapist later diagnosed me with social anxiety disorder, and I've been seeing that same therapist monthly ever since.

It's kind of laughable to me sometimes. A school dance or a speech or a party, those things terrify me. No amount of immersing myself in those things makes it feel any better, makes the tingling in my limbs or that rotten food feeling in my stomach disappear. Snakes, though? Spiders? As long as they're not poisonous ones, who cares? The dark? Love it. The natural world with all its mysteries and its dangers, it all makes sense to me. It puts me at ease.

People, though. They destroy me.

11

I cannot believe I got suckered into going *hunting.*

My dad hunts. He loves it. He goes out with his gun and his camo and sits in the woods for hours waiting for something to shoot at. I cannot think of anything that sounds more boring than that, to be honest.

I'm not doing quite the same thing. And actually, the sitting-for-hours-in-the-woods situation might be preferred.

"You won't have to actually *do* anything," Grayson told me yesterday afternoon. "We're just looking for cave insects, and everyone takes a turn being part of the hunting party, even Mary. I promise, it'll be fun."

And because I'm a totally pathetic human being who latched completely on to how nice he is and how cute he is, I agreed to join. He briefed me, a little, on what was going to happen, but it all sounded like science fiction to me. Something about ambushing a cavern of cave insects after a series of tunnels . . . I didn't listen as well as I should have. I just stared at his mouth while he talked.

Now, as the small group of us walks quietly along one of the tunnels with only a single torch for light, I think I should have asked more about what the hell constitutes a "cavern of cave insects." I mean, where was my scientific curiosity?

It's too late now, though, because we're supposed to be quiet while we travel. I'm not clumsy or anything, but I'm feeling a lot of pressure on this quiet thing and I'm worried I'll accidentally trip and ruin this for the whole group.

We squeeze single file through a narrow space. Grayson's before me; Alice is after. Grayson seems to be a regular with the hunting party, which doesn't surprise me, but I was a little surprised that it's also true of Alice. She wields a large, dangerous-looking knife carved from stone.

"It makes me feel like a prehistoric cavewoman," she explained to me before we left. "I'm no good with a bow and arrow, but I sure can stab things."

Grayson brought his bow, but he doesn't have many arrows, given the lack of materials, so he saves it for emergencies, he says. Like Alice, he carries a gigantic knife. I'm not carrying a giant knife *or* a bow, but Colleen gave me a small knife before we departed. She said she didn't think my ribs and I were ready, and Grayson argued that it was just walking and probably good for me, and I'm pretty sure she was mad when I decided to still go. But she gave me the knife.

My ribs *are* sore. But they're sore no matter what I'm doing, and I'm desperate to be part of things. I like working with Mary, but I'm afraid it'll make me seem less like part of the group to the others. I'm restless. Stressed. Anxious.

Alice touches her fingertips lightly to my arm when we're through the narrow space. I match my pace to hers so she can put her face near my ear and whisper, "Be extra careful from here on. This is where a bunch of tunnels meet."

I see what she means. This tunnel branches into several. We swerve down the second from the left—I make note in case somehow I get separated from the group—and continue to pass more branching off this one, like a network of limestone capillaries. There's a bit of a sulfuric smell here, different than the putrid corpse smell in the cavern. It gives me an irrational pit of fear in my stomach as I glance ahead at the torch bobbing with the steps of the man in front. Glenn, of course. They've obviously come down here before and know it's not a problem, but I'm picturing sulfur lighting up and killing us all with its toxic gas.

Glenn stops, and we all stop. There's a tunnel to my left, a gaping black opening and I edge involuntarily to my right. My shoulder brushes Grayson's and it distracts me, especially when he looks down at me and smiles.

The smile is short-lived. His jaw drops open, face contorting in horror as his eyes dart past my face. Fix on something in the tunnel.

I turn to look, too.

The breath leaves my lungs at the sight of the biggest spider I've ever seen. The size of a large housecat, easily. Bulbous body. Long, thin legs. Mouth-pincers twitching. Eight eyes staring.

Directly at me.

the spider

(not even close to life size)

12

I feel like I've come unstuck in time. My eyes are glued to the spider, and my brain's cycling through all the possible ways this could go—most of which end with the spider sinking its fangs into my body and sucking out my innards like a bowl of tomato soup. All the possibilities layer over one another while I stand, gaping at the thing, doing nothing to stop it.

Alice comes to her senses first. Her knife stabs downward in a swift, confident motion, sinking through exoskeleton just behind that nightmarish cluster of eyes. She holds on while the spider's legs dance and jolt. I want to be sick. I don't even *mind* spiders, usually. But this thing is unnatural.

When its death twitches subside, Alice pulls her knife free. She looks over my head at Grayson, smirking. "What is this, your first day?"

He looks sheepish and hurries to help another member of the hunting party who's knelt beside the corpse, wrapping the thing up in twine made of sinew.

"Thanks," I say to Alice. "For, you know, not letting me get murdered by a spider."

"Oh, it's nothing." She waves a hand dismissively. "They're disgusting, but they're not deadly."

"I, uh, should have asked what Grayson meant by *cave insects*," I say. "I figured they'd all be like the ones I saw Eleanor tear into the other day."

Alice laughs. "Spiders are actually not what we're hunting. They're kind of a pain, because you have to extract the venom glands before they're edible."

"Venom glands?" I arch an eyebrow.

"Hey." She holds up both hands. "All I said was that they aren't deadly. I didn't say it wouldn't hurt if one bit you."

I can't help it; I laugh.

And then the group is moving again. Like this spider thing is normal and no big deal. Grayson falls back into place beside me, his expression a little more serious than it was before.

They're all used to this. Experience things like this every day. The spider was a brief adrenaline spike and it's already over.

For me it isn't.

The spider might not have touched me physically, but it was another reminder of how completely different my world is now. Most of the time I'm cocooned by a fog of unreality that makes this all feel like a particularly vivid dream. But every so often, something *hits* and it's like a tornado blows through, decimates my life, and removes the fog in its wake so I can see every bit of the destruction.

My whole family thinks I'm dead.

I will never see them again.

I can't blame anyone for this except myself.

These three thoughts cycle through my mind more than any other since I've been down here. Especially that third one. I want to blame Sherri and Meg. And sometimes, I do. It's easier. In the end, though, it all comes back to: I could have said no. But I came anyway.

"Hey, are you okay?" Grayson touches my elbow with his fingertips. I'm torn between thrilled that he is voluntarily touching me, and the itchy panicky feeling I get when someone is close to me. "You're shaking."

I hadn't even noticed. My hands are trembling and my fingertips are numb. "I'm fine," I say, trying to sound confident. "It just happens when I get stressed."

"I'm sorry," he says. "Maybe Colleen was right and it was too soon for this, with your ribs and everything. I shouldn't have—"

"No, I wanted to come." I interrupt him *again*. I keep doing that, like it's totally normal and not at all socially awkward to just cut someone off when they're speaking. "I'm glad I came. I want to see this stuff; I want to be part of things. I just wasn't prepared, that's all."

Shame creeps up from my toes, and I'm glad, as ever, for the darkness of this cave and the fact that no one can see the way my cheeks burn when I'm flustered. I wish I was better at hiding my anxiety. It could be different with the people here. I could be

Regular Eliza, not Anxious Eliza. Except that I've already given too much away. They already know.

The tunnel we're traversing isn't the most interesting piece of cave I've ever seen. It's slightly downward-sloping, rocky, narrow in places, wider in others. No formations, really; nothing of note. I get pretty jittery now every time we pass a branch on the side where I'm exposed, even though Alice has shifted slightly, almost protectively, which I do appreciate. Alice doesn't always hang out with us. She's a little bit older—twenty-three—so she's not exactly a teen, but the next youngest adult is twenty-nine and Alice seems to feel more comfortable with the younger crowd than the older, most of the time.

"Are we going to a specific place?" I ask, voice hushed. Everyone else is being so silent.

Grayson nods. "There are a few tunnels down here that have high populations of insects. We're close."

Glenn pauses again, and thankfully there's no tunnel to my left this time. It's hot down here; sweat beads on my skin and I feel disgusting. Disgusting and heavy and compressed.

We veer left into an extremely narrow tunnel that widens out after a few minutes. It becomes quite bulbous, actually, and there are strange formations here. Instead of sticking up from the floor or down from the ceiling, they stab out from the walls. A hot, moist wind blows from in front of us, and I feel like I'm walking sideways through a set of jaws, the kind that could crush closed and grind me up at any moment.

The feeling isn't helped by a clicking noise ahead of us,

growing louder. I know I'm not actually *in* the mouth of some giant beast, but the clicking noise sounds like . . .

Well, like a giant insect, I guess.

"Get your knife out," Grayson says. He's tensed, fist clenched around his blade.

Suddenly, I want to laugh. It's actually next to impossible to hold it back, even though it'd be beyond inappropriate right now. It's just so insane—I'm in a *cave* and I'm holding a knife in my fist standing next to a boy doing the same, like a fantasy novel.

Only he's just a boy and I'm just a girl and neither of us is any kind of Chosen One and we're not on a quest. We're finding food, using the only weapons at our disposal, because we're desperate, and we're surviving. That's it.

The clicking grows louder, and I start to feel vulnerable. My ribs still ache and I'm no hunter anyway. What was I thinking?

"Now!" Glenn shouts, and everyone surges forward. Grayson told me to just follow the group and keep my knife ready and "stab the crap out of" anything that comes near me. So I follow.

Straight into a nest of the biggest insects I've ever seen.

Bigger, even, than the spider. They're the size of foals, and they look like a cross between a katydid and an ant. Their heads are ant-shaped, and so are their antennae, but their legs are long and curved and thin like a katydid's. They also have big, folded-back wings, except they're not leaf-shaped, they're . . . stone-shaped. These insects are meant to blend in here, I realize. They're meant to look like stalagmites.

It's one of the most surreal realizations of my life.

Until one comes at me.

It's got spines around its mouth that look like the sort of thing it might use to cage its prey.

And its legs have spikes that look sharp as saw blades. I'm in serious trouble if I don't move.

I do the only thing I can: I stab the thing directly in the mouth with my knife.

It doesn't die right away, but it does stop coming toward me. I try to pull the knife out, but it's stuck, so I twist and twist and twist until the bug's legs start to crumple and the mouthpart twitches seem less deliberate.

I look up then and meet the eye of Alice, who's looking duly impressed.

There were six more of these beasts in this section of the tunnel, and we killed them all.

Alice reaches my side in a few easy steps. She yanks out my blade and hands it to me. "Were you nervous?" she asks.

"Not at all," I say coolly, even though we both know it's a lie.

She laughs. "Admit it, though. This was pretty awesome."

I bite my lip, and then I confess: "I can't lie. It was awesome."

"How can they grow to be so *big*?" I ask, back in the colony. Eleanor and I are sweeping the floor of the main cavern. "Shouldn't their exoskeletons collapse under their own weight?"

Eleanor shrugs. "I don't think any of us could even *begin* to answer that question."

"During prehistoric times, there were dragonflies with six-foot wingspans."

I whirl around. Mary stands behind me, smiling patiently.

"But dragonflies have shorter legs, though," I say. "They don't really walk."

"True." Mary pulls a broom from a storage shelf carved into the wall and starts sweeping. "But they weren't the only over-sized insects that lived back then. I don't know what would possibly cause insects to grow so large down here, to be honest with you. Except that once one started, evolutionarily, the others needed to if they wanted to survive."

I mull it over. "So to survive the spiders, the katydids had to be bigger."

"I'm not a biologist," says Mary, "but it's what I assume."

"What else is down here?" I ask.

"Lots of things," says Eleanor. She seems eager to participate, now that she knows the answer to one of my questions. "Insects are the most prevalent. But there are also some mammals. Like the thing that attacked you, you know, when you first arrived. We call those cave wolves."

I shiver, remembering.

"And the firebreathers."

"What's that?" I ask. I'm picturing dragons, as anyone would.

"They're . . ." Eleanor pauses, thinking. "Well, they breathe fire. Not *literal* fire, but their breath can burn you. I think it's like an acid or something?"

She glances at Mary, who nods.

Encouraged, Eleanor elaborates. "They have fur but only on their chests and their faces, and a strip down their backs. They're a little bigger than a beaver, and they're a rodent. We don't see them very often; they seem to stay deeper in the tunnels."

"Wow." I push my broom more aggressively across the floor. "That's . . . something."

"It's a never-ending pit of wonders down here." Usually Eleanor's pretty upbeat, so her dark tone startles me.

"There are *some* wonders," Mary says, only she's being serious. "This system of caves is a feat of nature. It *defies* nature, really. It's also its own, perfectly preserved ecosystem, and we are a parasite, never meant to be here."

"You're saying that like it's fine," I point out. "But parasites are destroyed by ecosystems where they don't belong, or else parasites ruin the ecosystems."

"Yes," Mary agrees. "But it'll be interesting, won't it, to see which?"

The hair raises on my arms. I don't think it'll be interesting at all. Because from what she's telling me, there isn't a good ending. There's us destroying this cave's ecosystem—and then, let's face it, ourselves, when there's nothing left—or there's the ecosystem destroying us. Either way ends with us dead.

"We'll just have to get back to our correct ecosystem before anything too catastrophic happens, then, right?" I say timidly.

Mary smiles thinly. "That's the plan."

And I believe her.

I don't really have a choice.

Total number of people living in this cave: 13

Babies: 1—Stella (6 months)

Teens: 3—me (16), Eleanor (18), Grayson (17)

Adults: 9 (4 men, 5 women)—Alice (23), Mary (37),
Colleen (52), Maurene (46), Amy (29), Glenn (43),
Charles (32), Michael (66), Brandon (48)

Ways out: 0

13

Three days in a row, we have extremely successful hunts. I only participated in that first one; I'll take a turn again when I'm asked. But it put a twinge back in my ribs, and once I was freed from the adrenaline of the moment, I started to think about how much less cool the whole thing would have been had I died. Which feels like it could happen pretty easily, despite what Glenn says.

The only problem with several successful hunts in a row, however, is that the insects are starting to pile up. Colleen comes for me before I've even left my tent in the morning. I usually use the time between the wake-up bell and the breakfast bell to reread my journal and sometimes to write in it. But I've only read about two pages before the knock on my tent pole, and a moment later, Colleen's head poking casually inside. I shove the journal deftly under my pillow. I'm aware that there's no privacy or security here, so I don't write too much about the colony. Glenn wanted this journal when I first got here and that's always on my mind. So I've taken an "out of sight, out of mind" approach, hoping everyone'll forget I have the thing.

"You won't be with Mary this morning," Colleen says without preamble. "We need you to help the other youths dress the insects."

"Oh." I slide off my cot. "No problem."

Colleen smiles. "I didn't think you'd mind."

Breakfast is a quick affair, and then Eleanor and I are set to work on a pile of spiders.

"I thought we didn't prefer spiders because of the venom," I say.

"We don't," says Eleanor, "but if that's what we find, that's what we eat."

I wrinkle my nose. I've been eating insect for days now and I've gotten used to it. But gutting this spider, with its hairy legs curled crisply into its chest and its eight eyes still unsettling even in death, puts me up close and personal with my food in a way I'm not sure I'm prepared for.

"So with the spider, we have to extract the venom first," says Eleanor. "Other than that, the process is the same as any other insect."

I nod, nerves curling in my gut. I don't want to mess up.

Eleanor shows me where the retractable fangs sit within the mouthpart, connected to the poison gland behind it. Carefully, she cuts through the exoskeleton where the mouthpart connects to the head and pulls it gently free, bringing fangs and gland with it.

"But if you go too deep," she warns, "you'll cut the gland and the meat is ruined. Ready to try it?"

"Might as well be." I pick up a knife and grab a spider from the pile. The hairs covering its body are coarse but smooth, not as unpleasant to touch as I would have thought. I run a hand over one of its curled legs.

"Oh, and wash your hands in the river every few spiders," Eleanor adds. "Their hair can be an irritant."

I stop patting the dead spider at once, and Eleanor laughs. "I did the same thing, first time."

Cutting around the mouthpart isn't as easy as Eleanor made it look, but I am successful. After that, I set to work on the much simpler task of separating its legs and head from its body.

"How did you feel," I ask, "when you first came here? When you were first doing this?"

Eleanor pauses in the middle of slicing open a spider's underside. "I felt . . . Well, I wasn't happy." She presses her knife tip back against the spider's abdomen. "I was never an outdoorsy girl. The only thing I liked about nature was running in it. And look where that got me." She laughs, not unhappily. Eleanor, like me, fell victim to a sinkhole. Only she was on a running trail, not wandering around unstable swamplands. "I had a boyfriend back home. We met on the second day of freshman year. I cut him in the lunch line, and we argued. Every time I saw him for two months after that, we found something to argue about. And then, one day, right after I told him he had the stupidest face I've ever seen, he kissed me. We kissed as well as we argued, so we kept on doing it. We'd been together for over a year when I . . . disappeared."

I set aside the last of my spider's dismembered legs. "Do you miss him?"

"Sometimes, yeah. I try not to. I mean, he's gotta be someone else's boyfriend by now. He thinks I'm dead, and how long can he mourn me, you know?" She frowns, gripping the opening she sliced into her spider and prying it apart.

"What if you made it home?" I ask, because I can't help myself. "Do you think he would want to get back together?"

"Eliza," she says, exasperated. "There *is* no going home. I know it's hard to swallow right now but you *will* grow to love it here. I would never have touched a spider when I lived topside. I cried the first time I had to here. And now look at me. Pulling out the digestive tract like a pro."

To illustrate her point, she slops her spider's extracted digestive tract into a dented, ancient metal bucket at our feet. They found the bucket someplace, long ago. It's probably been down here since before my birth.

"I'm sorry." I stare at my spider's corpse, blinking back tears. I feel like I'm pushing her—*everyone*—away with my inability to stop asking *What if?* about going back to the surface. But even with the stray thoughts I have about staying, I don't understand how anyone can ever stop thinking about leaving. "I'm not being very respectful of your feelings, am I?"

"Oh please. Everyone who comes is like this at first. Grayson took nearly three weeks before he remotely settled in. He was like a bottle of pure fury. It's a miracle he didn't get kicked out, to be honest." She pauses. "And no, I don't think Clark and I could get back together in your hypothetical. Too much has changed. We wouldn't . . . I don't know. I've lived two years in a dark cavern, and he's spent two years thinking that his first serious girlfriend is dead. We've both had our own trials and they're such different trials, I don't know that we'd be able to grow back together."

That makes me feel pretty sad. The way she described him, their getting together, it makes me yearn. I've never had someone feel passionate enough about me to argue *or* to start kissing and never stop. I've had boyfriends, but they were short-lived and awkward romances. I hate that Eleanor doesn't think they would be able to have a happy ending. But I guess I understand it, too. I already feel so apart from my old life. I miss my parents and my sisters with the fiercest ache.

I don't miss Sherri and Meg at all. And I don't think that's a side effect of being in these caves.

"Have you, um . . . Has there been anyone down here?"

She laughs. "Well, since I'm straight, I've pretty much just got the one option who's within, like, fifteen years of my age. And I like Grayson so, so much as a friend. But we would *not* be compatible romantically. At all."

"What about . . . So have Grayson and Alice both also

been alone since they've been down here?" I hope it sounds casual, like I'm not asking with any ulterior motive besides curiosity.

Eleanor eyes me suspiciously. "Alice isn't interested in dating anyone." She brushes off her hands and pulls over her third spider. I'm still in the early stages of my second. "And Grayson, well, now there's *you*."

I blush fiercely. Thank God for the extremely dim lighting in this corner. "Yeah, but Grayson is so . . . and I'm so . . . I mean, we're probably incompatible, too."

"Really? You look pretty compatible to me."

I'm now breaking out in a stress sweat. "I, um . . ." I don't know how to finish that, so I just go back to my spider. I don't know why this, of all things, is spiraling me so much. But the idea that I might like Grayson and that it might be obvious enough for Eleanor to tell, even though I asked her pointed questions that are probably what *made* it obvious, terrifies me. What if Grayson can tell? What if he thinks I'm weird and then I'm stuck down in this cave with him *forever* and what if it's awkward for the rest of my entire life?

"Eliza," Eleanor says hesitantly.

I will my heart to stop beating so fast. It ignores me. "Yeah?"

"You have anxiety, don't you?" She says it gently and nervously, like she's not sure she should have brought it up.

Claws rake at my gut. I don't talk about this. "Yes," I admit, with a fresh flurry of nerves.

"Did you take medication for it, before you got here?"

I shake my head and realize that, somehow, talking about this is calming me down. "I've been going to therapy once a month since . . . seventh grade, I think? When my mom suspected that there was more going on with me than just puberty. I've been able to manage things pretty okay ever since then, so we agreed to forgo medication for now. If that changes, it'll be a conversation to revisit. Or . . . it would have been, I guess. Not so much now. And this is the most I've talked about this with anyone in a really long time."

I told Meg about therapy, right after I started going. But she had a lot of her own stuff to deal with. Sherri thinks anxiety is made up, so I never said anything about it to her, though Meg did once, when the three of us were fighting. We never discussed it again after that.

"I didn't mean to make you talk about it if you don't want to," Eleanor says. "I just . . . Please tell me if I do anything that makes it worse. I promise not to be mad if you do. I think sometimes my personality stresses out the socially anxious."

I laugh, even though I feel on the verge of tears. "No one's ever said that to me. I . . . really appreciate it." I swallow hard against the lump in my throat. "And I do not find your personality stressful, by the way."

And that's the exact moment when a cluster of insect eggs is dangled in front of each of our faces.

We both screech, involuntarily, and whip around to the laughing faces of Alice and Grayson.

"Our mantises were female," says Grayson, grinning broadly.

"And we are getting *really* bored over there," Alice adds.

"Come work next to us!" says Eleanor.

"We *tried* earlier," says Alice. "But Glenn felt that the four of us together would be *too distracting.*"

She rolls her eyes and air quotes those last two words. I glance across the room to where Glenn is also dismembering an insect. It must be exhausting to be so intense all the time.

"So do it anyway," I say, unsure where I have come up with this rebellious attitude.

Grayson glances down at me, still with that broad grin. I can feel Eleanor watching us and I get very nervous. "Let's do it," he says, and flings the egg cluster at me before taking off back across the cavern.

I pluck it off my arm and dump it unceremoniously into the bucket at our feet.

"It's like the colony version of receiving a bouquet of flowers, you know," says Eleanor, teasing.

"*You* are full of nonsense." I return to my spider. "And you're making me nervous. Like, regular-person-who's-trying-to-figure-out-if-they-have-a-crush-on-a-boy nervous. So I have to warn you, you may be in for a display of my truest social awkwardness pretty soon."

"Hmm, I might enjoy seeing that." She smiles. "Just kidding, of course. But be soothed in the knowledge that I have absolutely no shame and can one hundred percent out-dork you if I have to."

We're both giggling pretty hard when the others return, and neither of us can come up with a good explanation as to why.

For me, the explanation is pretty simple, though, and probably not at all what Eleanor expects: It's that, somehow, I've made a friend who wants nothing more than for me to be myself. And what a tremendous relief that is.

Cutting up insects to prepare them for a meal is a totally different process than the stuff we eat topside. The process, for posterity:

* Separate all the easily separated parts. Remove the legs & wings first (& antennae, if applicable), then sever the head. Leave the thorax & abdomen connected. Trash the head, wings & antennae.

* Cut legs into pieces at all joints & set aside. We cook these leg pieces in water boiled over the fire and then pull them apart when we eat them, like lobster. Minus the butter, so, you know, not nearly as delicious.

* Slice open abdomen. Extract some of their organs and other gross bits.

* Once all that's gone, just scoop out all the rest of what's in there. Or, depending on the insect, sometimes just spread the exoskeleton wide so that we can cook it over the fire as is and use the exoskeleton as a serving dish. It sounds like disgusting work, but it's... actually pretty fun!

14

Between the hunting trip and the fairly strenuous day of gutting insects (plus cleanup), I am paying dearly. I've definitely been pushing the limits on what my ribs are ready to handle. By dinner, I'm sore enough that I'm worried one of my ribs might be broken after all. I sit quietly, trying not to breathe too deep, while the others laugh and chat. When Eleanor asks if I'm okay, I tell her I just have a headache.

She accepts this and goes back to the conversation. I wish she'd realize I lied and press harder. It's a dilemma I find myself in constantly. I don't want to talk about how I'm feeling, don't want to let anyone know something's wrong. But I want them to, somehow, fix it for me anyway.

I want it to be effortless, like how Meg can use that soft, gravelly tone she gets when something's wrong, and instantly she's cocooned in sympathy. I don't know how to get people to feel like that for me. Not without making a fuss, and I'm not a fuss-maker.

After dinner, I'm on cleanup again. Amy, the woman who has a six-month-old strapped to her most of the time, is helping. I don't like to judge, but the baby makes me uncomfortable. Knowing that girl was born here and may never see the world where she belongs . . . Maybe I haven't earned an opinion on the subject, but it seems irresponsible.

Lifting a stack of stone plates into the washbasin brings a stabbing pain to my side. I drop the plates and crouch to the floor, catching my breath with difficulty.

"You all right?"

I look up. It's Glenn. Serious and joyless, as always.

"I'm fine." But the words crawl out from behind clenched teeth.

"You ought to take it easy." He folds his arms. "Those ribs are healing and you want to do it right."

"Yeah." I rise slowly to my feet. "I know."

"It'd be no good if you reinjured them." What a comforting man. So glad he's here right now. "We need everyone here as healthy as possible."

"Yeah." I edge away casually. "Maybe I'll go see Colleen."

"Good idea," he says.

But something about the *way* he says it sends chills crawling up my spine as I walk away. I've let myself begin to feel pretty safe here, in the confines of the colony. This is an excellent reminder that Glenn—and the others—don't need another burden. I'm sure he'd let me die just to use me for spare parts.

Colleen insists that I keep to minimal activity again for at least a couple days.

"Glenn's not wrong about the importance of everyone staying healthy," she says. "It's dangerous here if we're not at full strength. Better for you to rest and really heal up instead of half suffering and reinjuring yourself when you need the strength most."

"You mean like when we try to leave someday?"

Colleen stills. Her eyes go all giant and dark. "Eliza, honey, that's . . . not in the cards."

I twist my hands in my lap. "Why, though? All the ways people have gotten in, I—"

"Those aren't exits," she says quickly. "There are no exits. There is no way out. This is our home and you'd do well to stop talking about anything else."

I think about how this advice contrasts with Mary's. *Did you reread your journal today? Do you still want to go home?* Mary asks me those two questions every morning.

And then an odd sensation of doubt burrows into my brain. *Do* I want to go home? Where my friends are unkind and my world is confusing?

I shudder. Of course I do. *Of course.*

"What if people have escaped before, though?" I ask. "My town has that urban legend about the swamp and it seems like . . . why would anyone come up with that unless something triggered it? Like a person returning after a presumed death and claiming to have gone to the center of the earth?" My fingers itch to type this into my phone, look up old news stories about recovered missing persons. If only I could.

A shadow passes by the tent, man-shaped. Colleen's eyes flick up, fearful, for a moment. "You will drive yourself crazy thinking about things like that. You need to let it go. The sooner you accept that this is your life now, the better off you'll be."

"But—"

"Just trust me."

I think of all the times I've mentioned leaving and how it's been poorly received literally always. And it leads me to a terrible thought, something Mary keeps asking.

Are we trapped here because we're trapped here, or are we trapped here because this place has convinced us we don't want to go?

Sometimes Sherri is the most perfect best friend in the world. This is mean to say, but Meg can be exhausting. It's not her fault. It's just that every single day something is wrong that she needs me to fix. Whether or not I feel fixed myself. Sherri, on the other hand, never has anything wrong. She knows how to flirt, she gets good grades, her parents are lovely, kind people, and her brother is already off to college, leaving her with all the attention. She gives me gifts a lot. She'll order different types of gemstones off the internet and leave them in my locker at school.

At first, I loved that. It made me feel so special. Whenever I felt like Meg was slipping away, like Sherri was cooler than me and they were phasing me out, the gemstones were a reminder that Sherri did actually care about me, too.

But after a while, I started to get a stomachache every time I received one. Because it usually meant something was coming. A party I'd have to sneak out for, or a paper she'd need "proofread," or some other ill-advised idea.

I don't know. The gemstones didn't always come with strings attached. Maybe I'm not giving her enough credit.

But maybe I'm giving her too much.

15

My achy ribs are not great for my ability to sleep deeply, and I wake in everyone's sleeping hours with a soreness in my side and a full bladder. With a sigh, I edge out of my tent to make the journey to the outhouse. I miss real toilets.

But I love the cavern at night. Without the bustle of activity from the colony's residents, it almost feels the way a cave should. Quiet and dark and empty. The solitude is what I love about caves. The peacefulness. The raw beauty, unmarred by external forces. This cave is too lived in for all of that, but if I glance up at the stalactites on the ceiling, I can envision this place as it must have been before it was domesticated.

There's always someone on guard during the "night," just in case. Not everyone does it. I haven't been asked to, and maybe I should be insulted, but I am truly not guard material, so. I know who's on guard duty tonight, and on my way back from the outhouse, I stop where he sits.

Grayson jumps when I come up behind him and tap his

shoulder. I laugh. "A little jittery for a person who's supposed to be aware of their surroundings."

"The dangers aren't supposed to come from the middle of the cavern, you know."

I glance up at the many tunnels dumping into this room from the ceiling.

"I think I'd hear it if something fell from one of those," he says. "What're you doing, anyway?"

"Bathroom."

"Ah. I—" He stops, glances at something behind me. I turn slowly and see Mary emerging from her tent. "Quick," Grayson whispers.

He grabs my hand and tugs me into the darkness of the nearest tunnel.

"What—" He cuts off my question with a quick press of his finger to my lips. I couldn't speak now if I tried. Or move. Or breathe.

We both peer out of our shadowed hideout and watch Mary sneak down into the tunnel in the floor. The one that's caved in. The one we're not supposed to enter. She slides the hide back over it after she's disappeared, and I turn to Grayson for an explanation.

"I don't know what she does down there," Grayson says. "It really is caved in. I've seen it. But sometimes at night, she goes down anyway. I, um . . . She and I have a little agreement where I pretend not to see her."

"Why?"

"I don't know." He leans against the wall. "It seemed really important to her."

"Hmm." I glance over at the hole, drawn to it. If Mary can go down there . . .

"You think I shouldn't help her?"

"No, of course you should. I'm . . ." I hesitate. I trust Grayson as much as I can trust anyone I've known for such a short time and met under such questionable circumstances, but there's a sense of loyalty here that everyone seems to have caught except me and, by all appearances, Mary. And I don't mean loyalty to one another, but to the cave itself. "I want to see what she's doing."

Grayson raises an eyebrow. "You know that's a terrible idea, right?"

"I know. I want to anyway."

"I want to come, too."

"You . . . what?" I glance nervously around. "What if something comes in and we're unguarded?"

"One time in all the months I've lived here has something come during the night. Even this deep underground, creatures are wary of fire."

"Okay. Then . . . let's go."

Together, we sneak over to the floor tunnel. I'm absolutely exhilarated. It's the same feeling I get when I visit a new cave for the first time or when I see a really cool formation or I get a new type of rock. I'm about to *explore*.

There are steps carved crudely into the rock; necessary, given that the tunnel is almost vertical. Grayson climbs down first, all casual and relaxed, which makes me feel inadequate because once I've replaced the hide and enveloped us in complete and total darkness, I'm clinging on to the ladder with both hands and curling my toes in my sneakers, terrified I'll fall to my death.

It's not such a far descent, and at the bottom there's space enough for both of us to stand, if very close together.

"Hang on," Grayson whispers. He fumbles with something, and then there's a sharp click, and a tiny flame peeks out of the top of a lighter. "Do *not* tell anyone I have this. Glenn would take it away from me in a heartbeat. I don't usually use it; I just like having it. But I thought this might go a little easier if we had at least a *little* light."

"You came down here with a lighter?" It's not entirely uncommon for people to bring things like lighters into caves, just in case, but Grayson didn't fall into this cave prepared; he already told me that.

He grins sheepishly. "Have I mentioned that when I lived topside, a lot of the decisions I made were not great?"

I let it go. "I won't tell anyone you have it. I promise."

"Thank you." He holds out the lighter toward the wall to our left. Where there's . . . a half-blocked opening. "Well," he sputters. "That's . . . usually totally blocked."

As he moves the lighter closer, I notice something next to the opening. "Hang on." I grab his wrist and guide the lighter closer to it. A marking, three straight lines scratched into the wall. "How long has that been there?"

He shrugs, leaning closer to it. "Don't know. I've never noticed it before. But I've only been down here once. I was . . . I don't know if Alice or Eleanor or anyone told you, but I was pretty difficult when I first arrived. I was so mad. I think if I hadn't been young and strong, they would have turned me away. Anyway, I got obsessed with this tunnel and why I wasn't allowed in, and finally one day Glenn pretty much dragged me down here. He showed me the cave-in and then he shoved me against the wall and told me if I didn't fix my attitude I was gone and I would die alone wandering the blackness. Seeing the cave-in . . . I guess it was the wake-up call I needed, and I did chill out."

"But it's not a real cave-in, apparently." I realize I'm still holding his wrist and let go, blushing.

"Yeah." His voice shakes. "So I guess we'd better see where it leads." He goes first, stepping over the pile of unsettled stones, and then holding out a hand to help me do the same. I don't *need* the help, but I'm sure willing to take it. His palm is warm and calloused and it makes my heart race in a good way.

The tunnel is too narrow to walk side by side, so he stays ahead of me, but close. It's craggy and the low ceiling spikes with soda straw formations. Several sharp twists later, I notice that my eyes seem to be adjusting to the dark. Which shouldn't be possible. The darkness of a cave is a *complete* darkness, and even the faint glow of Grayson's lighter barely cuts it. Eyes cannot adjust to that. But now the walls ahead of us are faintly visible.

Grayson ducks under a jagged, low-hanging rock. I follow,

and on the other side, find myself in another cavern. A *glowing* cavern.

It's like gazing up at an alien sky. The walls, the ceiling, even the floor emanate a greenish, bluish light. Unreal.

"These are stones," I realize, running my finger over one of the glowing areas on the wall. "We could probably break some of these off and bring them back to the main cavern for light."

Grayson is still slack-jawed, drinking in the whole scene. "How did this . . . What . . . How could Mary not *tell* us about this?"

"Yeah, and where is she?" There's no apparent exit to this cavern, but she's nowhere to be seen. And it's *bright* in here. So bright. I thought Mary was my friend in this; I thought she was trying to help. But here is this whole cavern of brightness, so close to where we live, and we are existing by the light of two tiny fires.

"Look." Grayson kneels beside a large rock. "It's those three lines again. And there's an opening!"

I crouch beside him. It's not a big opening, maybe a couple feet in each direction. I wriggle into it. The other side is dark, but it opens up again. "It's another tunnel," I call back to Grayson. "And you can stand."

"All right. I'm coming."

A moment later, he stands before me. It's very dark here, with only the faintest glow of the cavern highlighting our outlines, and our nearness makes my skin tingle. His fingers brush mine when he reaches for his pocket. I hold my breath, imagining what it would feel like to kiss him. Just the *thought* is thrilling.

Especially standing so close to him that the warmth of his skin radiates toward me. The gentle sound of his breathing. I want to run my fingers through his messily chopped hair. The want is strong enough that I nearly do it.

But then the click of his lighter echoes, and the tiny flame appears like a barrier between us. He grins down at me and I smile back, but I'm a little shaken.

This tunnel is wider, and we walk side by side except when a stalagmite or other formation gets in our way. We're not walking long before we come to a fork. "Which way do you suppose she went?" Grayson asks. "Look, there's those three lines in this right tunnel."

"Yeah." I run my fingers over the three lines and then examine the left tunnel. "But look, this tunnel has a faint glow."

He joins me. Stands directly behind me so that his front is lightly brushing my back, and I don't move, but I don't understand how he doesn't feel my heartbeat through my spine. Is he standing so close because he wants to be near me? Or because I'm in the way and he's trying to see better?

"Let's try this tunnel, then," he says.

We go quietly, because the farther we get from the colony, the more likely we are to run into danger. As we walk, the glow gets brighter.

And then we stop dead, simultaneously, pressing ourselves into the wall.

This tunnel leads to another cavern filled with the glowing stones. Only this one is also filled with glowing *people*.

"Bioluminescents," Grayson whispers in horror.

"And *Mary*," I whisper back, pointing carefully.

She stands in the middle of the cavern, looking deep in conversation with a couple of the bioluminescents. But everything's so *quiet*. So many people wander about in the cavern, with luminescent skin, clawed hands, and an otherwise disconcertingly human appearance. But there's no crackling of flame, no voices, only the gentle padding of their bare feet.

Because they're not speaking with voices, I realize, they're speaking with *gestures*. The sign language Mary has been teaching me isn't something she made up. It's the language of the bioluminescents.

I give Grayson a tiny shove in the direction opposite the cavern. He takes the hint and we hurry back, all the way to the place with the glowing stones.

"What. Was. That." He paces the length of the small cavern. "What is she *thinking*, what is she *doing*? The bioluminescents—I heard they've *killed* people from the colony before. And she's been *visiting* them? I've been letting her come down here all this time. I thought maybe she just needed a place to be alone and to think. If I'd known she was doing *this*, I would have—"

He stops when I step in front of him. "It doesn't look good," I agree. "But we have to be calm until we know what she's actually doing. I mean, they were friendly with her, so that's a good thing, isn't it? I mean, they're *people*. There are probably some good and some bad, just like us."

"You're right." He folds his arms and lets out a frustrated

burst of breath. "But she still should have told everyone they were here and *told* us why she was teaching us this sign language. So I'm gonna stand right here until she comes back and she can explain herself."

"I don't think that's a good idea. Listen, I'm working with her tomorrow morning. I'll talk to her. If she has a good explanation, then fine. But no matter what, she has *no* argument against letting us *at least* come into this cave right here and getting stones. We could really use the light. I think everyone would love it, and it isn't fair that she's keeping it from us. I think—I wonder if maybe it'd help make people feel more like themselves again."

Grayson does not want to leave here and go back to the colony. He keeps shifting his weight and clenching his fists and my stomach ties into a knot because I hate confrontation so much and the idea of confrontation with Grayson makes me want to vomit.

"You're right," he says, surprising me. "I hate that you're right, but you are. *Promise* you'll tell me right away what she says?"

"I promise."

"Okay. Let's—we should go back, then."

I nod, and we start toward the tunnel that will lead us home.

I am a full-blown ice block the next morning when it comes time for my work with Mary. Confronting her from the very first second seems ill-advised, but I feel completely betrayed and I can't bring myself to talk to her normally at all.

"Did you reread your journal this morning?"

"Yup."

"And you still want to go home?"

"Uh-huh."

She narrows her eyes. "What is this attitude you've developed?"

My whole body tenses. "Tell me, how'd *you* sleep last night?"

"I slept very well. And you?"

"Not good at all. My ribs still hurt and I can't get comfortable. It means I wake a lot during the night. Sometimes get up to go to the bathroom."

I stop there, gazing levelly at her. When she doesn't respond, I continue. "It's interesting, what you see sometimes if you go to the bathroom in the middle of the night. Like maybe you see someone go down into the supposedly caved-in tunnel. And maybe you follow them."

Her expression changes now. Pure horror. "Follow them how far?" she asks in a low voice.

"The whole way." I fold my arms. "So. Got an explanation?"

"Yes," she says through gritted teeth. She glances nervously around. No one's nearby and the darkness embraces us. When she speaks again, her voice is lowered. "But you absolutely *cannot* tell anyone. Not a soul."

I hesitate, thinking of Grayson. I don't want to lie to Mary, but I don't want her to close up if I tell her I can't keep this secret. "I won't," I say, my limbs prickling with anxiety.

She glances around again. The cavern is not quiet. People

go about their daily tasks, laughing and talking in the semi-darkness. The baby's unhappy and shrieking. But when you're about to tell a secret, it always feels like your words will bounce off every wall and straight into the ears of people you want to hear nothing. "The reason I believe that we can escape by going deeper is because I *know*. Did you notice markings next to tunnel openings, below?"

I nod, a chill spreading over me.

"You said it before, Eliza. You believed that in order for a rumor to exist about a place where you can reach the earth's core, someone had to make it out to tell the story. And someone did. My grandfather." She slips onto her stool, pausing like she knows I need a minute for that to sink in. "He disappeared for over a year when he was in his mid-twenties and came back with a story about having fallen to the center of the earth. People didn't know as much about the earth back then, so he really believed, when he reached the mantle, that he *had* visited the earth's core. No one else believed even a sentence of his story; he was hospitalized for a psychotic break and he never spoke of it again until the dementia started in his nineties. I know people say a lot of things when their minds start to go, but when I would visit him, he described it all with such detail, such *clarity*. He told me all about the bioluminescents, that he'd lived among them for a time, that he'd wanted to stay. He lived here first, all alone, in this very cavern. And he left the markings to be able to find his way back when he explored. He didn't want to go home until the day he stumbled upon magma accidentally. He said it knocked him out of a trance. So, frantically, he retraced his steps and tried to make his markings clearer, leaving himself notes when he could so that he wouldn't forget that he wanted to leave. He hoped others would find the marks and follow them."

I narrow my eyes. "Except, we can't follow them if we have no idea they lead anywhere, because of fake cave-ins."

She sighs, squeezes her hands into fists. "My grandfather passed away five years ago, and I've been researching ever since. I have probably read up on every single missing person case in the state of New York, searching for ones that seemed relevant. I hoped I could find someone else like my grandfather. Someone else who had left. There wasn't anyone. So I decided I needed to come here myself. I found the bioluminescents before I found this place, and I still keep up with them, obviously. I'm hoping to someday get them to work with, to join together with, our colony here. The blockage in that tunnel looked to be a natural cave-in, I don't think anyone hid it on purpose. But I didn't tell anyone what was behind it, because I worried what they would do."

"You didn't think people would like to know that there was a way out?" I refuse to let her off the hook about this.

She laughs bitterly. "Of course I did. I'd found a different way here, and I was going to use it to help them get out while circumventing the bioluminescent village so they'd be left alone. All they really want is for us to leave them alone, you know. This is their home; it's not ours. Anyway, no one wanted to follow or even remotely believed me about another way out. I always try, and no one ever has."

I digest what she's saying, slowly. It's hard to wrap my mind around. "Why haven't you left by yourself?"

She scoffs. "It's dangerous, Eliza. *Very* dangerous." As much as I hate to admit it, I think I understand where she's coming from. Except for one thing: "You didn't tell me this when *I* came. Have you given up on trying to help others get out?"

"Absolutely not," she says emphatically. "No, I've just . . . changed my methods. Since the old way wasn't working so well for me."

I narrow my eyes.

"I told this story when I arrived," she said. "At least, part of it. I told them about my grandfather. None of them believed it at all."

"Well." My throat is dry. "*I* believe you."

Her lips tremble and I think if it weren't so dark, I would see tears in her eyes. "I'm sorry." She looks away from me, out over the cavern. "I'd forgotten what it feels like to hear those words."

"Did you tell Grayson this when he first came?" I ask. That'll make things easier. I won't really have to break my promise to her.

She shakes her head. "I had planned to. Grayson was the toughest I've ever seen to acclimate, and he has the sort of personality that makes people want to follow his lead. But he didn't settle into his fate slowly, like everyone else. One day he fought like a wildcat and the next he was a lifeless shell. I missed my window."

I frown. Grayson was the last person to arrive before me.

"Shouldn't you have told me right away, then? Instead of telling me to read my journal and being all cryptic?"

"No," she says vehemently. "Telling people too soon turns them into outcasts. The others become wary of you before they even get to know you. I had to wait; I just couldn't wait *too long*."

This sounds perfectly reasonable, but something about what she's saying seems off. She's telling me now because I found out her secret. How long would she have waited, otherwise? I think there's a part of her that wants me to know the truth, wants me to be able to go home. But I'm suspicious there's another part— maybe a stronger part—that wants me to stay. To be her geology student forever.

She was the person I trusted most down here. And now . . . now I don't think I can trust her at all.

"We don't have to tell everyone about the bioluminescents," I say slowly. "But they have to know about the stones. And if you don't tell them, I will."

"You do still want to leave, don't you?" she says. I can't tell what she's hoping I'll say.

"Of course I do. The stones?"

"Yes. I'll tell them."

"Good. And I'll work with you again once it's done."

Everyone is very excited about the stones. I, personally, am not so excited about how Mary tells everyone they were discovered.

"Eliza got curious and went exploring," she says. Colleen's disappointed in me after. She's the one who told me not to go down there, and I didn't heed her. Since she doesn't know *why*, it changes her view of me. She sees me now as a Mary clone—flighty and stubborn and unwilling to listen.

But that's fine. Because this whole thing has reminded me that I shouldn't trust Mary, either. Just because she's a geologist and she's taken me under her wing doesn't mean we have any kind of special bond. It makes me rethink . . . well, pretty much everything.

I do think that keeping the bioluminescents a secret for now is wise, but only because of that one thing she said: *All they really want is for us to leave them alone, you know.* We're pretty much aliens, invading a place that doesn't belong to us. The stories everyone tells about the bioluminescents don't paint them in the best light, but it's not up to me to decide their fates.

After Mary's announcement about the stones, Glenn leads the expedition into the cavern, because Glenn has to lead everything. He handpicks the people who will join him, and of course, I'm not included.

Once they've extracted a good quantity of glowite, we place them around the edge of the cavern, and use them to brighten the ill-lit half of the river cavern and the tunnel between. They're not a perfect substitute for fire, but they'd be better than nothing if we lost that light source. I shudder to consider the other repercussions of that, though. No fire means no cooking and no cooking means raw insect meat.

Plus, nothing scares away animals like fire.

"These are so pretty," says Alice. I sit with her and Eleanor on the bridge across the river, and Alice is running her fingertips over the surprisingly smooth surface of the stone.

The glowing bits are flecks, like how granite is speckled. The rest of the stone is a pale shade of gray.

"They really are," Eleanor agrees. Then she looks at me. "What's your favorite rock, besides this one? Like, what's the prettiest rock you've ever seen?"

I glance at the glowing stone. "I don't know. Not to be a complete nerd, but there are a *lot* of rocks I think are extremely beautiful. But I guess my favorite is tektite. It's so neat-looking, and also I love that we don't actually know if they come from space or from the planet." I hesitate, knowing that everyone hates talking about life above, but then I ask: "What careers did you guys want to have?"

"I had absolutely *no* idea," says Eleanor. "When I was a kid I wanted to be a vet, but then I realized that you don't just hug the animals better. I think I'd have an easier time cutting them open now that—now. But it still wouldn't be right for me."

"I wanted to be a fashion designer," says Alice. Her eyes dart off into the distance. "When I was little, I used to critique the outfits of all my friends. I'm sure you'll all be shocked to hear that they did *not* love it."

"I might've appreciated it," I say. "My fashion sense as a small child was *bad*."

Alice laughs. "Mine, too. I had *no* room to be judging anyone."

I glance down at what I'm wearing now. Jeans and a T-shirt.

Most of the people here are still wearing whatever clothes they arrived in. We have a stockpile of spares, from those who brought them, and things that have been found on scavenging trips. A few have taken to wearing furs. Alice's jeans are pretty distressed at this point. They look good on her, but eventually they're going to fall right apart.

Alice could pull off furs if she had to, but I don't think she'd like it.

"How long did it take before you decided you would rather stay here than try to go home?" I ask.

"I don't think it was really a conscious decision," says Alice. "After a couple weeks, I basically acclimated. There isn't a way back, and sitting here thinking that there is leads only to misery. Besides, this is home. This is where I belong."

"What if there was a definite way out?" I ask. "Like, what if one day a scavenging group came across a big hole and you could see the surface and could just walk right out. Would you go?"

Alice shrugs. "Sure, I guess."

"Probably," says Eleanor.

Neither one of them sounds at all convinced. And I know, deep in my heart, that I'm running out of time before the apathy takes me, too.

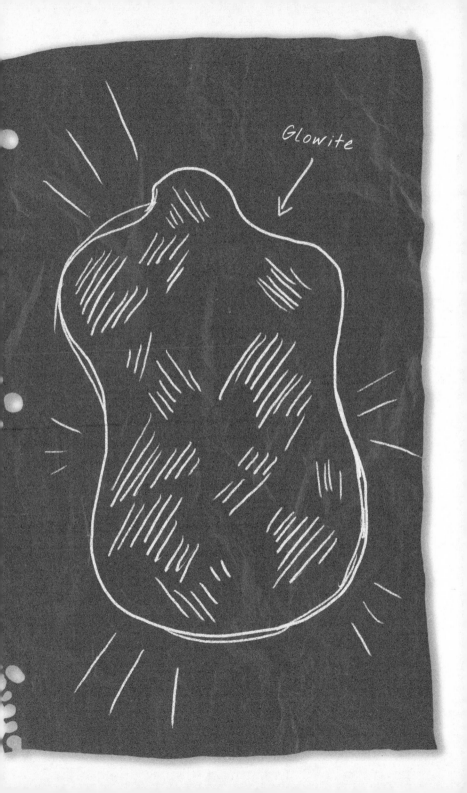

16

I wake during our resting time, and something feels *wrong*. I can't place what it is, and I wonder if it's actually morning. But it's too quiet for that. No voices, no laughter, no sound of breakfast cooking over the fire. I sit up, blinking in the steady, gentle light of the stones. Maybe that's it; the stones' light has been unsettling me since we placed them. I'm not used to the additional brightness, to feeling so spotlighted. Usually it's only the flickering orange of the fire. *Flickering orange* . . . The only light shining through the flaps of my tent is green. My fingers clench around the fur blanket that covers me.

I sit up. My cell phone's still tucked under my cot; I've had it off since I arrived, so it should have some battery. It powers on, but it's low. I get a weird feeling in my stomach about that. I knew eventually the battery would die, but seeing it in front of my face with the sad eleven percent remaining makes it more real. I flick on its flashlight and emerge cautiously from my tent.

There, where the fire should be, is a smoldering pile of

embers. A few adults have crowded around it, and they glance up at the light from my phone's flashlight.

"What's going on?" I ask. My fingertips tingle like they do when I feel like I'm injecting myself where I don't belong, but curiosity and fear defeat social anxiety at the moment. Mary's not one of the adults crouched around this fire, but Colleen is. I step closer to her. "Does this happen sometimes?"

Colleen's brow furrows, the lines harsh under my phone's light. "This has never happened."

I swallow. *"Never?"*

She looks down at the coals, and I follow her gaze. This fire didn't just burn low.

It was put out.

I glance around with frantic eyes. Who would do this? What purpose would it serve? My gaze rests on something in one of the side tunnels. I squint and lower my flashlight. Still there. A faint bluish glow.

"What is that?" I point.

Beside me, Colleen rises slowly to her feet. "Go back to your tent," she says quietly. Ominously.

Going back to my tent would be the smart thing to do. But my tent is a lonely triangle of gloom and I just—don't want to go. I shake my head.

"Eliza—"

I ignore her and walk cautiously toward the blue glow. It's almost neon. There's a bioluminescent person hiding in that tunnel and I don't care how dangerous they are; I *have* to see

them. I have to know what they want, whether they came on
their own or were brought here by Mary.

Colleen catches up to me, Glenn right at her heels.

"It's one of those people," Glenn says.

"Yeah, I figured that out." I keep walking. "But I want to
see why they're here."

"Eliza, you are too young and this is *not* safe," Colleen says
sharply.

"You're not my mom," I snap. Quietly, because the blue
glow is starting to tremble and I don't want to scare them away.
Yet. "We're *all* living out the rest of our days down here; it's not
more dangerous for me than for any of the rest of you."

Glenn pulls out his sword—I don't have to look behind
me, I know it by sound. It's made of stone, and he crafted it
painstakingly himself; at least, that's what Grayson told me.
Every time Glenn returns from a hunting expedition, he sits down
with the thing and cleans it lovingly, ridding it of insect guts
and gore.

I still can't see the bioluminescent. But the way the glow is
flickering, I can tell that they're terrified.

"Wait," I say to Glenn and Colleen. "Please, just wait."

I don't know if either listens, but I pick up my pace to leave
them behind anyway. I reach the tunnel entrance, and I stop
dead.

This is my first time seeing a bioluminescent up close, and it
shocks me. *Humanlike* is the only way to describe the person

huddled before me. They have the general appearance of a person, the same overall body shape and facial structure. The eyes are quite large, the skin translucent. A full head of light-colored hair falls around the being's face, and a shift in movement tells me I'm looking at a woman. Or a girl. It's hard to tell age because the neon-blue glow of her skin haloes her and hides details. Well, hides details in one way, exposes them in another. Because I can see her innards like an X-ray.

Her bulbous, unblinking eyes bore into me even as she quakes, hunched into herself. Her fingernails, I notice, are long and sharp. And suddenly I realize how foolish this was, to come into this tunnel knowing this other being was here and not knowing what she might do to me.

She inhales noisily and reaches out a hand. I jump back.

Mary's voice shouts something; the commotion's finally woken her. But she's too late to fix this situation.

Within moments, hands on my shoulders pull me out of the way as Glenn and his sword lunge forward.

"Glenn, *don't*!" I scream. His sword pushes up into the woman's rib cage, through the crimson, beating heart. Blood bursts through the woman's insides, spreading like an inkblot, spotlighted by the glow of her own body.

"What's she holding?" Colleen asks, peering over my shoulder.

Glenn kneels beside the corpse, unwrapping her fingers from something. He holds it up.

It's a plant—glowing, just like the woman. A slightly more purple color, but basically the same. The realization hits me like a fist in the chest.

She wasn't going to hurt me at all.

She was trying to give me the plant. To give me a light.

And now she's dead.

When I was eight years old, I found a monarch butterfly. I caught it under a jar, and then transferred it to a bug cage that I'd filled with grass and sticks and a little container of water. At first, my butterfly seemed happy there. But it wasn't long before it died. I was completely distraught, and my mom (who is not great at the whole sympathy thing sometimes) explained to me that monarch butterflies don't eat grass.

I hadn't meant to kill that butterfly. I thought grass was what it ate, I thought it would be happy in the little home I'd made for it. But I felt terrible anyway. Sometimes, it really doesn't matter what you intended. It only matters how it ended.

17

Introvert time is hard to come by when you live in a cave. People are everywhere. Which isn't so bad, now that I'm used to it. But every once in a while, I need to be alone. Especially with the ghost of the dead bioluminescent lurking over my shoulder.

My alone spot is the far side of the river, in a corner where the firelight doesn't reach so well. There's a cluster of cave formations here. Mary refers to it as "the grove," which is perfect. The little formations do look like plants. Blobby mushrooms, spiky grasses, bulbous tree stumps.

It sounds dorky, but I like sitting here with my little miniature stone forest. It gives me peace. I had a *spot* at home, too. When my house got too loud from its family of five. Or my life got too loud from best friends who never thought I was enough.

There was a small hill to the left of my house, and on the other side of the hill, what I called an "almost cave." It really wasn't a cave at all, but it was a spot where a few large boulders formed a shelter. When I was little, I used to build cities there, out of smaller stones and twigs. Not to brag, but they were pretty excellent. I got older and my interests changed, but I never stopped going to my quiet spot. With a book or my headphones or my journal.

If this cave weren't a tomb, I'd think this new spot was even better.

Last night was beyond horrible. I've never seen anyone die, and I never wanted to. I don't have the stomach for tragedy, and I don't know how to be around anyone right now. Glenn didn't have to do what he did, no matter how he justifies it. He came up to me afterward and told me he was sorry I had to see that but he was glad he was there to save me.

I only nodded. I didn't tell him it was the bioluminescent who needed someone to save her, not me.

Mary wanted the plant. I know she thinks it was meant for her, and probably it was. But she couldn't get into it with me in front of everyone without blowing her secret, and everyone who witnessed the incident told her to let me keep the plant. They all think I'm fragile now.

At least I've won their sympathy back.

I glance up at the sound of someone approaching. It's Grayson, and I can't decide whether or not I'm glad to see him.

"Hey." He shoves his hands into his pockets. "Mary asked me to have you meet her in the glowing cavern."

I sigh. "What does she want?"

"She didn't tell me, but I'm going to guess it has something to do with the bioluminescent and the plant she gave you."

He holds out a hand, which I take, even though I don't want to see Mary right now.

"You want to come with me?" I ask as we walk back toward the main cavern.

"I wasn't invited."

"So what? *I'm* inviting you."

We stop in front of the now-open tunnel in the floor, and he stares at me for a long moment. "You don't want to be alone with her?"

I shake my head. He can interpret that however he wants. That I don't feel safe, that I'm mad at her, whatever. Anything he guesses is probably a little bit true.

"Then okay." He gestures to the rock ladder. "Ladies first."

As we travel down the tunnel, now lit with glowite, I swallow a lot of things I want to say. Finally settle on something that's not too loaded: "Is it weird when a new person comes?"

"Sometimes, I guess. You're only the second person who's come since I've been here, so I don't have a lot of experience. But yeah, you have to adjust and make a place for them in the group. We're such a small collection that every addition has a ripple effect, changes the entire dynamic."

I frown. "That sounds bad."

He laughs. "I guess, but it isn't. We were all new once, you know. Even Colleen. Why are you asking?"

"No reason."

We walk in silence nearly the rest of the way to the glowite cavern. Then Grayson's hand lightly grips my arm. "Eliza."

I turn. He tilts his chin down so that his lovely green eyes meet mine.

"I think your ripple effect has been an especially huge one. I'm sure not everyone's pleased about that. But we have sat here in stasis for so long; we need someone like you to stir things up."

"How am *I* going to stir things up?" My voice comes out regular, which is a miracle considering my heart is clogging my throat. "I've never stirred up a thing in my life."

"I don't know why you think you don't matter." He gestures to a glowite stone. "You literally brightened our existence."

My cheeks burn. "Okay, but that was really all Mary, you know. All I did was threaten her a little."

"Just take my cheesy compliment and let's go." He shifts his weight and I realize *he's* blushing, too.

"Okay. I accept your cheesy compliment."

"Thank you." He spins me by my shoulders till I face the glowite cavern.

I slip inside, where Mary waits, looking impatient, near the cleverly covered exit on the far wall.

"Eliza, good. Come over here!"

I reluctantly join her at the wall.

"I'm *really* not at all enjoying this little teenage pout you've developed," she says.

"And I'm not enjoying the way you're referring to my legitimate anger as a 'teenage pout,'" I fire back.

"That girl wasn't supposed to come when she did," Mary says. "That plant, it's a peace offering. The bioluminescents exchange them when two villages negotiate peace. She should never have tried something like that without me. And now . . ." She shakes her head sadly. "Now it's over."

"Her *life* is over," I say. "And the rest of them must be so angry. Are we even safe anymore?"

Mary opens her mouth but says nothing.

"Yeah." I squeeze my arms across my chest. "That's what I thought."

"She brought the plant for me," Mary says stubbornly.

"And she *gave* the plant to me. Right before Glenn murdered her."

"This wasn't my fault," says Mary quietly.

I'm all ready to lash out at her again, but then I notice the tears in her eyes and I soften. Mary befriended this community of bioluminescents and now they'll hate her. *Our* community thinks she's a complete oddball. I can relate to how alone she must feel sometimes.

I want to blame her for ruining our safety here, but our safety isn't what's been ruined. It's the illusion that's shattered, the one I crafted so carefully to delude myself.

"How sure are you about the way out?"

"Well, I haven't followed the trail myself, not the whole way. But I'm very confident."

I nod, shove my hands into my filthy pockets. I don't look at Grayson, because I can't. He's my best hope at a traveling companion, but I told him everything Mary said and he still seemed . . . unenthusiastic. I don't want to push too hard and make him dislike me altogether, but I can't do this alone. I can't.

"How are we supposed to trust you?" Grayson says, so softly. "You've told so many lies."

"I have," Mary says. "I've done a lot of things wrong. I want you to leave because it's the right thing to want. It's my role, the reason I'm here. But also . . ." She shrugs, meets my eye. "Sometimes, when you find people who just *fit*, it's hard to let go. I'm not perfect. It's been . . . It's hard to let go."

I swallow a lump in my throat. "You know I have to, though. And I have to do it soon, or else . . ." I do brave a glance at Grayson then, my fingertips numb with anxiety. He still looks torn, but there's something in the way he looks at me. Something . . . hopeful. "Or else I may never get the courage to go."

I think it's the wrong thing to have said. The spark of something in Grayson's expression flickers and dies, replaced with a slight frown.

"I know you do," says Mary, oblivious. "And in my heart, I hope you do. Both of you. And anyone else you can convince." She's silent for an uncomfortably long moment, then, "She was my friend, you know. The bioluminescent woman."

"I'm sorry." I don't know what else to say. What happened was a needless tragedy born of Glenn's inability to hold himself back. I think about him and that sword, the obsessive way he cares for it. The way he needs to participate in every hunt, every scavenging mission. Everything that involves leaving the colony.

"Glenn would never hesitate, would he?" I ask. "If he thought there was a threat to the colony, from inside or out, he would take care of it and not ask questions."

It takes Mary a long time to answer.

"I think you've seen," she says, "exactly what Glenn is capable of."

There is nothing so far removed from us
as to be beyond our reach, or so hidden that
we cannot discover it.

- René Descartes

18

Glenn catches Grayson and me as we're emerging from the tunnel. He asks us to please see him in his tent, and he uses the same voice teachers use when they want to talk to you about a piece of homework you did terribly on but they don't want to embarrass you in front of everyone.

Grayson and I exchange a concerned glance, but we follow him.

Glenn's tent is a lot bigger than my tent—or anyone else's—and made of nylon. It's stocked with things he's confiscated "for the group" but appears to be keeping all to himself until completely necessary. My eyes are drawn immediately to my backpack, stacked in the corner with some others. And my headlamp and my flashlight are perched atop a pile of light sources.

"So, given that she's nowhere to be seen at the moment, I'm going to take a wild stab and assume that it was Mary the pair of you just met with down in the glowing cavern," says Glenn, cutting right to the chase.

"Yeah, she asked us to," says Grayson.

"I've noticed, the past couple days, that you seem to be spending less time working with Mary, Eliza."

I shrug. "There's a lot to do. It doesn't always make sense to spend my mornings on geology stuff, as interesting as it may be." Then, even though my body thrums with anxiety, I have a bold moment. "And I know Mary and I may seem really similar, but there are aspects of our personalities that don't always mesh. So sometimes . . . I don't want to be around her."

"What aspects of your personalities, if you don't mind me asking?"

"I kind of . . . *do* mind, sorry." Who even am I? Glenn frowns at my answer, but I hold my silence, and his gaze. I cannot feel my hands.

"That's fair," he says finally. "So about this morning's meeting, though—"

"It was about the plant," Grayson bursts out. "She still thinks she deserves that plant because she's our resident scientist. But the bioluminescent gave it to Eliza, who's *also* a scientist."

Glenn sighs. "Mary can be a lot to take sometimes, as you now appear to be aware, Eliza."

I nod, though I don't like that he's talking about her this way to me.

"She means well, but she's very set in her ways, gets obsessed with things easily. You'll learn, over time, when to decide whether it's easier to just give in to her whims, or whether it's something you should hold firm on. This one is your call. But I'm just letting you know, giving in may be easier."

"Yeah," I say, though I have no intention of giving Mary that plant. "It might."

"Well, I won't hold the two of you up any longer." Glenn smiles and it's probably meant to be friendly, but his smile is as intense as everything else about him. "Just wanted to check in, make sure that Mary wasn't being . . . wasn't trying to coerce you into anything you didn't want to do."

We're outside his tent and across the cavern before Grayson turns to me and says quietly, "*That* was weird."

"Yeah." I frown, run fingers through my knotted, oily hair. "I think he suspects she's trying to convince us to leave."

Grayson sighs. "He could just *ask*, instead of turning it into the Spanish Inquisition."

I laugh, even though I don't find his joke—or anything, really—all that funny at the moment. Thankfully, Grayson is understanding when I excuse myself back to my tent. The tent doesn't provide me the same sense of serenity as the grove, but I feel restless and unsettled and I'm not sure where I want to *be* right now. Seeing my things in Glenn's tent settled a feeling like bad food in my gut, and I don't even know *why*. I still have my journal and my phone. Those were the most personal items I brought.

I slip the journal out from under my hide and start to read it. I haven't in a couple days, and it's become a comforting part of my routine that I don't want to depart from. As I skim my words, some more interesting upon reread than others, I feel *off*. It's a crawling sensation under my skin that I can't identify. A sense that something is out of place but no clues as to what.

And then I reach a page from three days ago. I read it. I read it again. And again.

I slowly close the journal, my breath catching hard in my lungs, because I've figured out what's wrong. Three days ago, I wanted to leave here with every ounce of my being.

Today, my brain knows I have to go. But my heart could be content here forever.

You have a mom and a dad and two sisters. You have friends. You have school. You like the sun and the moon and the stars. You want to look at rocks from all over the world, not just from New York. You want to go to college. You cannot trust Mary because you don't understand her motives. You cannot trust Glenn because you understand his motives too much. You are not safe here and not happy here and you KNOW THAT. If you start to forget why you know that, then read yourself this paragraph every day, Eliza, and remind yourself that there is only one thing you need to do:

FIND A WAY HOME!!!!

19

I have been underground for two weeks now. Two. Weeks. The time has passed in a series of scratches on the side of my bed and notes in my journal. I barely trust my measure of time, but without it I would already have lost track. Two weeks might not seem like much. It sure isn't when it's the last stretch of summer vacation, for example. But here? It seems like an eternity.

"Eliza!" Eleanor gestures to me from across the cavern. I abandon my work with Mary's collected geodes to join her by the fire. Because it's our turn to cook lunch today.

"Katydid or millipede?" she jokes.

Because, obviously, the answer is millipede.

They live deeper in the caverns than the katydids do, and they're harder to kill. Their exoskeletons are rock-hard and they can move so fast on their million little legs. Well, not *little*. The millipedes down here are about eight feet long. Remnants of an earlier time, when insects roamed the surface of our earth in unimaginable sizes, as Mary likes to remind me. A time before even the dinosaurs.

And I don't know if it's because I've already forgotten what regular food tastes like, but millipede meat is *good*. It has a rich, nutty taste and a good moisture level. Not too dry, but also not like a pasty glob of overcooked rice.

Anyway, we got a few of them yesterday, and it's all everyone wants to eat until the meat's gone.

"So when are you and Grayson going to do something?" Eleanor asks as we scoop the meat from its storage container onto the thin slab of rock it's going to cook on.

My cheeks burn. "What are you even talking about?"

"*Please*. You know exactly what I'm talking about. He flirts with you all the time."

I brush this off with a wave of my hand. "It's just because I'm new, which makes me temporarily interesting."

Eleanor rolls her eyes. "You're permanently interesting. And what was up with you bringing him with you to talk to Mary the other day? Like he would have gone if he didn't like you."

"Well, if something's going to happen with Grayson," I say lightly, "there's no *way* I'm going to be the one who initiates it."

"What if he keeps flirting with you forever and *never* kisses you?"

"Then we don't kiss."

"You exasperate me," she says, but it's with a smile.

I wonder what would happen to Eleanor and me if we left this place. Would our friendship remain intact, or would we fade? We get along so well. Like Sherri and I do, when Sherri's not being so . . . Sherri-like. Eleanor's a window into the sort of person Sherri could have been if she hadn't thrust herself into the role of alpha friend so aggressively. They have a lot of similarities. Bossy, funny, confident. But Eleanor knows when to stop. She has empathy. She's become my closest friend. Maybe the closest friend I've ever had.

You're supposed to want to leave, my brain whispers to me.

Because, of course, I *don't* want to. But I feel wrong about that. It's the reason I've decided to stop being angry with Mary. I need her asking me if I'm reading my journal (I am) and if I still want to go home (I don't). I need to confidently lie in answer to that second question in order to feel right about things.

I prod my spatula into the meat, moving it around like scrambled eggs. Eleanor does the same thing at her end. We work toward the middle and then work back. It's not too tough of a job, to be honest, especially since everyone takes turns. And it's kind of nice, the way we all eat together at each meal, like a big family.

"Colleen! Injury!" The shout comes from the far end of the cavern, near Mary's workbench.

My heart flies to my throat. Wordlessly, Eleanor and I lift the stone off the fire and set it aside so the food doesn't burn; then we both rush over.

It's Alice. She's sobbing and curled into a ball, and I can't tell how badly she's hurt but blood slicks everything she touches, so I'm guessing it's pretty serious.

"What happened?" Colleen asks, trying to peel Alice away from herself.

"Bioluminescents," Alice gasps. Colleen gets her stretched out, finally, and I stare in horror at the heavy scratches across her stomach and ribs. "I didn't expect—hadn't gone very far. They're *never* up this way; they don't usually . . ."

She stops to cough, and then starts weeping, curling up against the pain. Colleen's eyes flick up and land on me. Since I'm the first one she noticed, I'm the one she commands: "Get my supplies."

I run to do as she asked, heart thudding against my tonsils. I'm only gone a couple minutes, but the crowd has multiplied to just about everyone who lives here by the time I return. I barrel through them and hand the bag to Colleen.

"Wait, I'm gonna need help," she says when I start to back away.

I freeze in place while she rummages. She pulls out a chunk of moss and presses it over the rib wound. "Can you hold this here for me?"

I kneel beside Alice, pressing my fingers as gently as possible onto each edge of the bandage.

"With pressure," Colleen instructs. I press harder, and avert my eyes when Alice flinches and groans. "I'm going to have to sew this up, so hold on to that while I get the needle ready."

This is not the kind of science I'm interested in. I don't want to watch Alice's shredded abdomen get sewn back up.

"So they just attacked you?" I ask, doing my best to focus on her eyes.

"Yes," she whispers. "I mean, not right away. I think—I don't think they expected me to be alone. And when they realized that I was . . ."

"How many were there?"

"Three. I don't think . . ." She bites her lip. "I think if they meant to kill me, they would have. I think it was a warning."

"A warning about what?"

Alice notices then that others are starting to lean in, and she shakes her head. It doesn't matter, anyway, because Colleen has the needle ready now. She tells Alice how much it's going to hurt, and gives her a cloth to bite down on. I hold her hand because it feels like the right thing to do, but I don't watch as the needle dips into her skin with no anesthetic at all. She crushes the bones of my fingers with bruising force, but it's a bearable pain.

And while her screams fill my ears, blocking out everything else, I think about what she said. I think about *my* bioluminescent, the woman who was just trying to give me a peace offering. How scared she was, how I knew immediately that she had no intention of hurting me.

A warning.

Because we killed one of theirs, and we went from neutral to enemy in the blink of an eye. It's Glenn's fault. He's too kill-first-ask-later. And it's Mary's fault, for not trying sooner to make us allies. But it's a little bit my fault, too.

And I can't help but feel afraid that I've accidentally endangered us all.

Alice finds me later, when I'm sitting cross-legged on the far side of the river. I washed my hands and arms of blood a while ago, and afterward . . . I couldn't bring myself to go back to the main cavern.

"You okay?" I ask.

She sits beside me with a grimace, dangles her feet in the water. "Not my best day."

"I'm surprised you're even up and about."

"It pretty much hurts the same no matter what I'm doing, so I might as well do what I want." She offers me a half-hearted smile.

"I'm so sorry, Alice, I feel terrible about this."

"*You* didn't claw me."

"I know." I curl my hands, nails digging into the rock. "But I can't help feeling like if I hadn't approached that bioluminescent, the one Glenn killed, we wouldn't be in this situation. Where we're, like, working up to a war or something."

"It's ridiculous, isn't it?" Alice stares out over the water. "We're miles below the surface of the earth, and we still can't stop ourselves from starting wars. Are we fundamentally flawed as a species or what?"

I laugh humorlessly. "I guess we are."

I stare at the water. Orange flame reflected in its surface, flickering violently.

"Do you ever feel . . . buried alive?" I ask, still watching.

"Sometimes I feel like this place is a coffin and I'm screaming and screaming but there's too much space between me and anyone who could hear it and dig me out."

I can picture it in my mind, more vividly than I want to describe. When I really let myself think about it that way, it feels like my bones are cracking under the weight of all that's above me. Like my lungs are running out of air, and my heart is running out of time.

She doesn't say anything, so I go on: "We're going to die if we stay here."

"I know." Her hands squeeze into fists. Unsqueeze. Squeeze. "Can I . . . Never mind."

"Can you what?" I prompt.

"I . . ." She swishes her feet slowly back and forth in the water. "I did something that might upset you."

"Oh? What's that?" My stomach roils.

"I read your journal."

My jaw drops open.

"Hear me out," she goes on quickly. "It was only a couple days ago. After Glenn killed that woman. I started to feel sort of . . . I don't know, wrong, I guess, and I wondered if you knew anything about it that you hadn't told us. Which you didn't, at least not that you wrote. But reading it . . . I saw how bad you wanted to leave here, and I remembered things I haven't remembered in months. My home. My family. Wanting to leave."

She stops there, inhales sharply. I glance up at her, my heart beating fiercely.

"I want to leave," she says. "This is not our home, and we don't belong here."

"I want to leave, too." I say it in a rush, like I have to speak it aloud to make it true.

"Okay. Um . . . what do we do now?"

"We see if anyone else will come with us, and then we just . . . go?"

"I think we need to do this fast. Like, tonight. Before we forget again and lose our nerve."

I nod, and rise to my feet. She's right. This place, it wants to keep us. And it makes us think we want to stay.

Alice struggles a little bit with standing up, so I bend to help her. As I straighten back up, I see something in the shadows of the cavern's corner that makes my blood run cold.

Glenn.

Meg has always been the friend who needs the most attention. The one who has things always wrong. And I've been the friend who doesn't quite get it because "your family is perfect, Eliza," even if sometimes the manipulative things Meg's mom did to her felt a lot like the exact things Meg did to me.

When we were younger, sometimes I would try to talk to her if something was wrong. But Meg always had something that overshadowed it. She and Sherri sympathized for about a half hour in ninth grade when I thought Terry Milburn liked me and it turned out he...super didn't.

But then Meg had a text fight with her older sister and started to cry and just like that, I was alone with my heartbreak and had to be strong for Meg at the same time.

Eventually, I didn't tell them so much about the things that made me sad. Their non-reactions made it much worse than dealing with it alone.

But now I think I'm done with that. I don't think I want friends who need me when they're sad but can't be there in return.

I deserve more. I will ask for more.

20

He steps out when he sees me looking at him, my mouth agape in horror. He's wearing his sword at his hip. His face creased with his ever-present serious expression.

"You can't ask people to leave," he says bluntly.

"Why not?" I fold my arms. This confrontation plucks at all the anxious parts of my brain.

"Because they won't go. They don't *want* to go."

"They *do*," I insist. "We're all just brainwashed and need to be snapped out of it."

As I say the words, I realize how true they are. I feel *awakened* right now. Plugged into reality. And I don't know how long it will last.

"Alice," I say through gritted teeth. "We need to ask everyone now."

She nods agreement.

Glenn grabs my arm roughly. "You don't know what a mistake you're making. You don't know everything you think you do. This cave wants to keep us, but it can't do that on its own."

"Let go of her." Alice's voice is dangerous. "She's right. We're going to ask everyone and we're doing it now before you can stop us."

Glenn releases my arm. "You're young," he says harshly. "And *foolish*. You think I'm trying to intimidate you, but I'm trying to *save* you. I—"

"Save the thinly veiled threats for someone else," Alice says coolly and takes my hand. "Let's go, Eliza."

And we do. Glenn doesn't follow.

Eleanor sees us at once. "What's the matter?" she asks, pulling us to the side. "You both look like you just had a run-in with a cave wolf."

"Something like that," I say. My whole body trembles, fighting panic. "Listen, we need to get everyone's attention, like, right now."

"Everything okay?" She slides an arm around my waist.

I absorb the comfort of her gesture. "It will be."

"Well." She grins. "I'm loud. I'll get their attention."

She accomplishes this in the most obvious way possible: by climbing up onto one of the seats around the fire and shouting, "Eliza needs everyone's attention over here immediately, please!"

Her voice echoes around the cavern, loud enough to make me flinch. Seems like the sound could practically carry on down to the bioluminescents in their own little village not far below us.

Once everyone's staring at me, I start to feel very sweaty. How am I in charge of this? I look to Alice, but she just smiles encouragingly.

My voice wavers when I speak: "This cave wants to keep us here. It has us convinced we belong, but we don't. Some of us will live longer than others, but none of us will make it as long as we should. That baby?" I gesture toward the infant, whose mother, Amy, pulls her closer. "She'll never see the sun. Never go to school. Never play sports or have fights or go away to college. Not if she stays here. But she could do all of it. This is not our home and we can leave it."

Everyone gasps, and I, myself, am just as startled. I'm saying the words and part of me believes them, but another part whisper-screams *NO*. This is my home, and my words are wrong.

"How?" Eleanor asks.

I blink, dazed. "What?"

"How could we leave?"

"Oh, um. We would go deeper. And then when we got closer to the mantle, we would hopefully find a fissure or something that leads to the surface. The earth's crust is actually not that deep; it's unlikely that the distance between the surface and the mantle here is more than twenty miles. Anything leading to the surface is probably much straighter than the tunnels we've been traveling through. It wouldn't take us too long from there, at least not comparatively. Am I getting that right, Mary?"

Mary looks startled that I mentioned her. "Yes, I believe so. Of course, we wouldn't know for sure until we got there."

Helpful.

"So anyway, I, um, that's my plan. Alice is coming, too. The rest of you are welcome. You just have to snap out of the grip this place has on you."

I've said the wrong thing, and everyone is angry, shouting at me. They're silenced by a shout from Colleen that rattles the walls. She steps to the front of the group, eyes flashing.

"You think," Colleen seethes, "that you, a child, are going to come in here and tell us what to do?"

"I'm not! I'm telling you what *I'm* going to do. But I wanted—"

"Eliza. Dear." Colleen steps closer. Her voice has changed, sweeter now, but anger still rages behind her eyes. "It's natural to want to go home at first. You still haven't been here that long. It took Grayson longer than this before he was ready to stay, didn't it, Grayson?"

When I started talking, Grayson wasn't really that nearby, but as this has progressed, he's moved closer, now leaning against the wall only a few feet from me. Our eyes meet for a moment, and his are filled with indecision. He already knows this plan. He just has to get on board. "Um, yeah. It took a while."

"It won't take you much longer, I promise. Until you understand, truly, how wonderful it is to be here. You love caves, don't you?"

"Yes." My entire body vibrates with stress.

"And you love the friends you've made here? Alice, Eleanor." She pauses, and her voice takes a more conspiratorial tone. "Grayson."

I bite my lip, and nod. "But they can come, if they want. I hope they do come."

"What about me?" Colleen says, her tone almost hurt now. "Haven't I treated you almost like a daughter? Wouldn't you hate to leave me behind?"

My heart punches my throat, fist-like. "I would. I'd feel terrible." *Be strong, Eliza.* "But you could come, too."

"You would give up all of this, all of *us,* on a *chance?*"

"I would. I believe Mary when she says the odds are high." My voice is barely a whisper. "You're not the only people I care about. My parents and my sisters and my friends at home think I'm dead. I can't just live here, knowing they're home, devastated like that."

"Are they, though?" Colleen arches an eyebrow. "Are they devastated?"

I open my mouth to say yes, but it doesn't come out. Are they? Maybe Sherri and Meg don't miss me at all. Maybe they're relieved I'm gone so it can be just the two of them, the way they've clearly wanted all along. And my family . . . they love me. I know they do. They'll be sad, they *have* to be sad. Unless—

"Of course her family and friends are devastated," says Eleanor, hooking her arm in mine. "How could they not be?"

Tears prick my eyes. I shake my head to knock away Colleen's words.

"If you would leave us, you're a *fool,*" says Colleen, turning dark again. "And you're certainly not taking anyone else with you."

"Yes, she is," Alice cuts in. "Eliza and I decided this together."

"And I'll go with her, too," says Eleanor firmly.

"Me too." Grayson pushes off the wall and moves to my other side.

"So a third of the colony is just going to *leave*?" says Maurene. She certainly never cared whether or not I was here before. We've barely spoken this entire time. "You can't *do* this to us."

Others begin chiming in angrily, feeding off the foundation Colleen built. Working themselves into a frenzy. They're so loud, so furious. I can't even understand what they're saying. And they're closing in on us slowly, firing up a panic inside me.

Glenn chooses that moment to stroll casually past. All smug, watching this go down exactly as he said it would.

"Anything to add, Glenn?" Colleen asks as he approaches his tent.

"I think you've got it covered," he says and then disappears behind the nylon-zippered opening of his tent. It strikes me as very out of character for him to miss an opportunity to point out how right he is.

"Eliza," Grayson says quietly right at my ear. "This was a bad idea."

"Yeah," I whisper. "I'm seeing that now."

Slowly, I step back, trying to pull myself out of the spotlight. Of course, there are no more shadowed areas in here, thanks to the glowite. My limbs feel weak and my stomach wants to expel everything I've eaten today.

"Where exactly do you think you're going?" Colleen lunges

toward me, grabbing at my arm. "I thought you were a nice girl, Eliza. I thought you were fitting in so well. But you're poison. Odd, like Mary, but worse because Mary doesn't try to turn our colony against itself."

I search out Mary with my eyes. She's frowning at the back of the crowd. I have one of those moments where I truly feel for her. To be used constantly as an example of what's not good enough. She has made mistakes, sure, but she's done as much for this community as anyone. She's helped everyone understand the environment they live in; she's told us all how to get back home; she's come up with ideas to build better cots and to keep fires lit longer and more efficiently. But because she's different, because she cares too much about the geology and the hunt for discovery, they all hate her. No matter what she does. She can't win.

Just like you can't win with Sherri, my brain whispers, like now's the time to be thinking about *that.*

"You could all stand to be a little bit more like Mary," I say coolly. "And if you don't think I'm fitting in anymore, then kick me out."

"Oh no, absolutely not." Colleen's grip tightens on my arm. It hurts, but I grit my teeth and keep my expression neutral. "You're dangerous, Eliza. You cannot be allowed to roam these tunnels unfettered."

"But I—"

"Into the tent," Colleen commands, shoving me toward my tent. "The rest of us will decide what's to be done with you."

And much to my surprise, she doesn't throw me into the tent alone. She shoves all four of us in there.

For a long moment, we stew in stunned silence. Eleanor beside me on my cot, Alice standing near the tent flaps, Grayson sitting on the floor.

"What do we do now?" Eleanor whispers.

"That depends on what they think they're going to do with us," I whisper back.

"They've moved away, I think," says Alice. "Colleen pinned this shut somehow so I can't see anything, but their voices are really faint."

"I am so sorry," I tell them. "I had no idea."

Eleanor squeezes my knee and rests her head against my shoulder. "*I* had no idea that I wanted to leave. So that's something."

"Yeah." Grayson's brow furrows. "It's strange. I fought so hard when I first came here. I was *sure* I was being trapped. The only thing I would talk about was going home and no one wanted to hear it. Lately, though, I feel myself missing home. And it . . . it *hurts*."

"That's how I've been feeling, too," says Alice. She brushes a curl out of her face. "Ever since I read Eliza's journal."

"You did *what*?" Eleanor is scandalized.

"Don't worry about it. We're fine," I say. But I do pull out the journal and hold it to my chest in case anyone gets any wild ideas. "What we need to do now is just figure out how to leave without getting them all worked up again."

"Where are they, exactly?" Grayson asks.

"I can't tell." Alice pries at the tent flap again, but it won't come open.

"Hang on." Grayson rolls onto his stomach, edges toward the loose bottom of the tent. He peers beneath it for several seconds. "They're in the tunnel by the river cavern. I think if we sneak around the back of the tents, we could get pretty close to our escape before they've got a chance at spotting us."

"And what do we do when we *get* to the escape?" Alice asks. "Not to be a Debbie Downer, but it's in the middle of the room—they're gonna notice."

"We'll have to run," says Grayson.

"We have no food," Eleanor points out.

"Nah, but we know where to find it." Grayson pulls out his knife. I have two beneath my bed, and I retrieve them both.

"And no light," Alice adds.

"We have to go through the glowite cavern," I say, and I move to help Grayson, who's cutting a slit up the back of my tent. Once it's long enough that we can all slip through, he puts away his knife.

"Ready?" he asks.

"Have to be." I shrug. He places a hand on my back. I take a deep breath and slip out the back of the tent.

Colony daily routine:

* ~~Wake up. Figure out if it seems like other people are moving around, or if it's still night.~~

* ~~Get dressed and come out of my tent.~~

* ~~Breakfast. (I'll help cook each meal approx. once a week.)~~

* ~~Morning activities—I "intern" for Mary, some people go hunting or scavenging, others clean.~~

* ~~Clean the cavern. It's always dirty. Total lost cause. Something to do, though.~~

* ~~Lunch, when the hunters return (or when people are hungry if they take too long).~~

* ~~Help gutting the insects. Apparently I'll do this approx. 4x per week.~~

* ~~Hang out with everyone OR have alone time OR help Mary with stuff.~~

* ~~Dinner.~~

* ~~Clean up dinner.~~

* ~~Hang out till people start going to bed.~~

* GOING HOME!!! ☺

21

We've made it down about half the length of the cavern when Mary appears.

"Thank God you're still here," she whispers, glancing over her shoulder. "You're heading down the tunnel, I assume?"

My throat goes entirely dry. I don't know whether Mary can be trusted, but she's seen us, so I have to hope. "Yeah."

"Okay." She glances back again. "You don't have long. Here's the situation. They know the bioluminescents are unhappy with us now, and they're planning to use you as a solution. Keep you tied up until the bioluminescents attack us, and then use you as human shields. Eliza first, the rest of you if needed. Colleen has utterly lost it; I've never seen her like this." Confusion crosses her face. "I didn't realize—the cave is keeping us here, but Colleen is, too. She feeds into it. The isolation—it's all—never mind, that's not important now. What's important is that you escape. And I'm going to help. Get to Glenn's tent. It's nearest the tunnel. Then wait for my distraction. They'll all pay attention to me, and you can flee then. Okay?"

"Sounds good," says Eleanor.

"You can't come?" I ask wistfully.

Mary shakes her head. "Your life is above, Eliza. Mine . . . I guess it no longer is."

"How're you going to distract them?"

Mary smiles. "By telling them some truths I've been hiding."

And she's gone before I can say goodbye. Watching her retreating back tugs on something deeply sorrowful in my heart.

"All right," says Alice. "Let's go."

We edge forward again, creeping toward Glenn's tent. "Look," I whisper when we arrive. "My backpack."

It's sitting next to Glenn's tent, off to the side, hidden from the view of the tunnel, where everyone's currently discussing us in heated voices. Glenn stands near the back of the group. My fist closes around the strap of my bag, and I swear, as I recoil into the shadows, he meets my eye and nods.

That's when Mary distracts them. Her voice carries all the way over here. "I befriended those bioluminescents and *you all* ruined it!" she screeches.

And suddenly, everyone's swallowed by the tunnel. Following her deeper in, would be my guess. I don't have time to think about it. "Go," I hiss. "We have to *go*."

We surge forward, ripping the hide off the entrance to the tunnel. I let the others go first; they all throw themselves down as quickly as possible. When I follow, I grab the edge of the hide in my fist and yank it back in place over my head before I start down the ladder.

And then I pause, glancing up at the blackness over my head. We've left the colony for good now; there's no going back, no second-guessing. The finality of it hits like seeing that first shovel of sand thrown onto a coffin at a funeral.

This could be *my* funeral.

That fact is more real to me now than it ever has been.

I take a deep breath, steady myself, and descend.

The earth is made up of four layers.

* Inner core: The actual center. Made up of nickel & iron. Totally solid, unbelievably hot.

* Outer core: Nearly as hot as the inner core. Made up of nickel & iron. It's liquid, though.

* Mantle: Much larger than the other layers. It's made up of magma, which goes from hard at the top to soft and melty at the bottom.

* Crust: The outer layer. The one we're in now. It's the thinnest layer, and the only one we are really able to access. Though the crust is especially thin at the bottom of the sea, and the mantle would be more accessible there. By machines, of course.

22

We're a somber group. All of us, probably, are letting our doubts get to us right now. I feel like there's a target on my back. Colleen could notice our absence at any moment and lead the others after us. She wants me dead now, and that's hard to swallow.

If Mary's wrong about the marks leading to a way out, I'm out of options.

Our only light source is a few chunks of glowite we pry off the walls—one for each of us, and a couple backups, which I stuff into my bag. I'm surprised to find that it's not empty.

"Glenn packed this," I say, shocked. "My headlamp is in here, plus my first-aid kit, two empty bottles, some clothes, some food . . ."

I don't have time to rummage around too deeply right now, so I just stuff the glowite and my journal inside and slip it back over my shoulders.

"So Glenn . . . helped us?" Grayson says with wonder in his voice.

"Apparently."

I don't have it in me to think about that right now, so I don't. I push my backpack ahead of me and squeeze through the low opening out of this cavern and into the tunnel beyond. Alice and Eleanor follow quickly, Grayson last. He does his best to replace the stone that covers the opening, but it'll be easy for anyone to find once they know we must've gone somewhere.

As we continue down the treacherously craggy tunnel, I think about how much I've changed, physically, since I got here. I've always been thin; it's my natural build. But now I'm *strong*. This would have been work before. Now it's nothing. My arms and stomach are starting to have definition. My lungs have stamina. I'm in great shape.

If I could figure out how to bottle up everything I've learned and sell it as a workout, I'd be rich.

The tunnel is jagged and unpolished. Every time it narrows, I get terrified it'll close up. Or that Grayson won't be able to squeeze through the craggy walls.

Several times, we have to turn our bodies sideways, but then there's a stretch that lasts for over five, difficult minutes. To my left, Eleanor's breathing grows more and more ragged as we continue.

"You okay?" I ask. It's a whisper, because we don't know what else is down here.

"Just feel like I'm being crushed. Nothing to worry about," she responds dryly.

"Got it." I keep going, wincing when sharp spikes of rock scrape my skin, and wincing harder when I hear Grayson, up ahead of me, let out a guttural curse word.

When the passage finally opens up, we find him crouched with a hand pressed to his shoulder blade.

"What happened?" I ask, lifting his hand to look at the slice. It's not too long, but pretty deep.

"I'm too big, is what happened," Grayson mutters. "Rock took a bite out of me."

"Okay, well, I think I can patch it up. But you're going to have to take off your shirt for a second."

I hope it's dark enough that no one can see me blushing. Whether he can see my embarrassment or not, Grayson grins. "You know, I get told that a lot," he jokes as he pulls the shirt over his head.

"Of course you do." I roll my eyes. And avert them from his torso, which, obviously, I've seen before when we've gone swimming. But I've never *commanded* to see it.

"Let me help," says Alice. "Colleen actually taught me some stuff."

Between the two of us, we get Grayson patched up with minimal gauze. I'm feeling pretty good about it. My first wound.

"Okay." I stand, hands on my hips. "You can put the shirt back on now." With a smile, I add, "Now, how often do you hear *that*?"

He grins sheepishly. "Unfortunately, about as often as I hear the other thing."

We all laugh. It's tense, because we're doing something terrifying, but it's also something I haven't noticed or felt since we came down here: hope.

What feels like several hours later, we make camp in a small cavern that branches off the tunnel. It's as safe and well protected as we're going to get. Eleanor and I arrange our glowite in a line across the door, giving us the illusion of a barrier. Predators probably won't feel the fear at the sight of our glowite that they would if we had a roaring fire, but that's not really an option, so oh well.

"I'm so happy." Eleanor settles into a corner, running her fingertip over a thin stalagmite.

"Yeah? How come?"

"Because we're *doing it*. We're leaving. I'm just—" She breaks off, swiping at her eyes. "Sorry, I just can't even *believe* it. I can practically smell the outdoor air. I can't *wait* to go home, and see my mom and my brother and, like, be a person again. I have so many goals for my life, so many *dreams* and none of them revolve around being kept like a hostage in an underground cavern. You know, I don't even really *like* caves. I guess I appreciate them more now, but I've never even been, like, the tiniest bit interested in them. Yet here I am, living in one. I know we've got a long ways to go and I know things are going to get tough, but I'm so glad we're doing this. It's like the act of simply moving forward somehow broke whatever spell I was under."

I smile at her. "I'm glad we're doing this, too. And I'm glad you're here with me." I pause, biting my lip. "You're my best friend, Eleanor. The best friend I've ever had. I don't know, maybe that's dorky to say. But it's the truth."

She squeezes my hand. "I feel the same way." She lies out on her back, hands behind her head. "I'm going to lay like this under the sun first moment I can."

I mimic her, staring up at the craggy ceiling. "I don't think I remember what the sun feels like."

She sighs contentedly. "I definitely remember. It feels like pure joy getting absorbed into your skin."

"Pure joy," I repeat, and close my eyes.

The deepest anyone has ever drilled into the earth's crust is about 7.5 miles. This wasn't even a person, mind you, it was a drill. The temperature had reached something like 350 degrees Fahrenheit. The mantle is usually 20-30 miles below the surface (if you started on land).

And it's not just the temperature that increases, it's the pressure, too. We should have all been crushed long before we had the flesh melted off our bones.

Mary estimates that we are currently at least 10-15 miles under the surface. And the temperature is hundreds of degrees lower than it should be. The difference in pressure from the surface, barely noticeable.

If we step outside this anomaly for even one second, we are dead.

23

On our second night, Grayson and I volunteer to hunt. I don't know what's gotten into me. Volunteering to go kill some cave insects, all confidently.

We bring my headlamp and a couple knives. And we set off cautiously to look for an enclave of insects. *Without going too far.* Alice actually pulls out a mom voice when she tells us this.

Unfortunately, we *do* find an enclave of insects, down a narrow, questionable side tunnel. But the insects are . . . not what either of us were expecting. They're enormous—no surprise there—and have jaws like a soldier ant's on fat, cricket-like bodies. I think one could saw me in half before I could blink.

"Abort mission," I mutter to Grayson. *"Now."*

We back out of the tunnel slow-quick in our movements, praying nothing heard us.

"Should we go on?" Grayson whispers, uncertain.

"I don't know. If that's what we're gonna find . . . it seems like the two of us shouldn't be hunting alone."

He nods. "I agree. Let's go."

We're about halfway back to the group when my headlamp starts flickering. And then dies.

My mom would make me lick a bar of soap if she heard the word I utter when it happens.

We're alone in this unfamiliar tunnel and it's pitch-black. Not an ideal scenario.

"Well," says Grayson into the darkness. "At least we weren't in the tunnel with the insects when *that* happened."

I appreciate his optimism. "Yeah . . . as long as nothing followed us. Or *starts* following us."

His hand finds mine in the darkness. "We'll be fine so long as we don't get separated."

Okay, then.

"Is this the right thing?" I don't know what makes me blurt it out like this. If it's the darkness making me bolder, or if it's his fingers laced in mine or what. "I'm scared that—I'm worried we will all die and it'll be my fault."

He's silent for a moment. Then: "If we all die, we won't care if it's your fault."

"Grayson." I stop walking, tightening my hand around his so he doesn't continue on without me.

"It's Colleen," he says. "And this *place*. Getting inside your head. Leaving was right. It's *time*."

I wish I could see his expression. This darkness is so oppressive. "Good. That—well, I guess I've always had you on my side about this, huh?"

A low chuckle. "Yeah. And I don't plan to quit now. You're

always . . . It's funny because I know you love caves, but there's something about you, Eliza, that feels like the sun."

I might not be able to see him, but I can feel the heat as he turns to face me, hands slipping to my waist. It makes my whole body feel like a bonfire.

"I think you're really pretty, you know," he says, close to my ear.

I don't know what to say. Don't have the beginning of a clue how a non-awkward person would respond to that. So I don't try to respond like a non-awkward person. I say the first thing that comes into my head. "Are you talking to me, or to the tunnel wall?"

He laughs, and tightens his hands on my hips. I reach out until my fingertips meet solid flesh. Skim up, along the side of his neck until my fingers twist in his hair. My heart is beating so fast, it's going to break open my rib cage pretty soon.

And then our lips meet, and even though it was me who pulled our faces together, I'm still surprised when it happens. His hands leave my waist, sliding over bare skin as he moves them up my spine. I draw in a sharp breath, pulling him closer to me and kissing him with all the force I possess.

His mouth leaves mine and delicately traces the curve of my throat, leaving shivering skin in its wake.

Confession: I have only ever kissed two boys before now. One of them was even more socially awkward than me, which meant that after our (not-very-good) kiss, we never spoke again. Neither of us could summon the courage. The other was at one of the parties Sherri made me attend, during a game of spin the bottle. He put his whole tongue in my mouth and it took everything in me not to retch.

This is not like that at all. This is the opposite of that. It feels natural and easy to slide my fingers through his hair, down his cheeks, along the twist of muscle in his arms. I'm not usually confident about anything when it comes to people, but I'm confident about this.

Our mouths collide once more, a little harder than we mean to, and he lets out a small laugh. I smile. He can't see it, but he can tell when he kisses me again and my lips are curved.

This is perfect, I think, and then I echo the sentiment aloud.

He rests his forehead lightly against mine. "I agree."

I swallow the urge to ask him a million questions about why on earth he likes me, *me* of all people. Why my personality isn't off-putting, why it's fine that I'm so into rocks, why he doesn't think I'm weird. Because it doesn't matter *why* he likes me. I know that he does, and that's enough.

I slide my arms around him, holding tight. My face fits perfectly beneath his chin. His fingers slip through my hair with a contented sigh, and there is something so nice about just *existing* like this. I tilt up my chin so we can kiss again, and this time, we don't stop. I'm pushed back against the wall of the tunnel, one of Grayson's hands between the back of my head and the hard stone, the other on the small of my back.

I can barely breathe, but I don't care. I don't care about anything but this, us, together.

And then something bumps against my leg.

Something, I realize with horror, that is not any part of Grayson's body.

"Grayson." The horror is evident in my tone. He stills. "We . . . are not alone."

"Insect?" he whispers.

The thing at our feet growls, as if to say no.

I'm not proud of what happens next. But . . . I flee. It's beyond cowardly, and I *know* that as I'm doing it, but I do it anyway. The sound of heavy breathing catches up to me, and I want to scream and scream and scream.

A hand slips into mine. The breathing is Grayson. "Don't slow down," he says.

"I—"

"Don't apologize. *Run.*"

I don't apologize. And I run.

There's a pinprick of light ahead and the *only* reason I haven't smacked face-first into a wall is because this tunnel is fairly straight. My elbow's scraped the side several times, though, and this feels like my first flight all over again.

We stumble, wild-eyed, back to our campsite. Eleanor and Alice jump up and hurry over to where we've collapsed in a heap of heaving breath and terror.

"Bioluminescents?" Eleanor asks, hand on my shoulder. I shake my head. Look to Grayson, because I don't even know *what* it was.

"Firebreather," Grayson whispers, and the others recoil. He holds out his foot. The bottom of his pant leg has been singed.

Guilt swoops down, heavy and cloying.

"I thought it was one of those dog-creatures," I say, my voice cracking.

"I thought so, too," says Grayson. "When it growled. But then it . . . well, did this."

"Doesn't look like it got your skin," says Alice, inspecting closely.

"No, it didn't." Grayson sits up. His voice is tight, not from pain, but from worry.

This is extremely sobering. Our first dangerous encounter since our departure, and a good reminder that we're not safe.

Our eyes meet but I can't keep contact. This is, of course, exactly what would happen to me. Have the best kiss of all time interrupted by a creature that spits acid.

It's the least of my worries right now, but all I can think is, *Grayson is never going to kiss me again.*

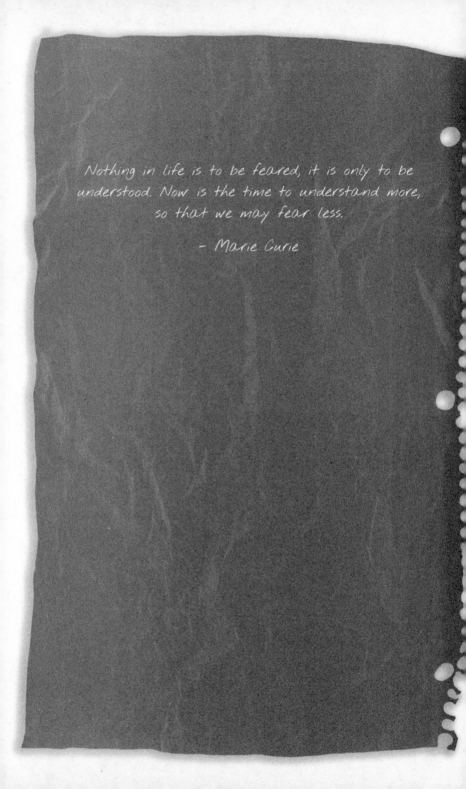

Nothing in life is to be feared, it is only to be understood. Now is the time to understand more, so that we may fear less.

– Marie Curie

24

I am a big chicken, so I avoid Grayson for the rest of the night and as long as I can the next day. *Avoid* is kind of a strong word, because it's literally impossible to avoid someone when you're traveling in a group of four through treacherous, creature-infested tunnels, but I am *never* alone with him.

Until he corners me.

Nicely.

We've stopped in an L-shaped cavern to take a break, and I'm hidden off to one edge, scribbling in my journal by the light of my plant. He saunters over casually and plops down beside me.

"Maybe I'm being paranoid," he says, resting his forearms on his knees, "but it seems like you haven't wanted to be near me since we kissed."

I say nothing, which, I guess, is as much a confirmation as anything I could've said.

He nods curtly. "Was it . . . Did I do something wrong?"

"No! No, definitely not." I close my journal and tuck my legs under myself. "I'm . . . I didn't want to pressure you."

"Pressure me into *what*?"

I shrug and look away. "Into . . . anything."

"That is not helpful."

He sounds frustrated, and, I mean, I can't blame him.

"Grayson, I'm sure this is not news to you, but you are extremely good-looking."

"Okay."

I almost laugh at the way he just *accepts* what I said. But there's an undertone to that *okay*. One that says, *Please elaborate.* "That was my third kiss. Ever."

"Well, it was my second. So there." He sees the way my eyebrows have risen to my scalp and rolls his eyes. "I'm not any better looking than anyone else, you know, it's just been a while since you've seen what other guys look like."

I snort. "I've been here like two weeks, Grayson. Anyway, I'm just not sure . . ." I hesitate, because I'm about to sound like a huge loser, but I'm already kind of being one, so I might as well go all out. "I don't know why you would like me enough to . . . I am really bad at social situations, and I have no idea how to navigate this one."

He lifts my chin with gentle fingers. "You could start by kissing me again. If . . . only if you want to."

I don't hesitate; terrified he's going to change his mind, I lean in and brush my lips lightly over his. It sends tingles through my body that have nothing to do with anxiety, for once.

His hand grips my knee and he kisses me back. Suddenly, I think I remember what the sun feels like. It feels like *this*.

Spreading warmth across my skin and settling happiness into my heart.

"Can I tell you a secret?" he whispers, lips grazing my earlobe.

"Of course."

"You keep implying that you don't know why I'd like you. But I think it's *much* more surprising that you like me."

"Please." I trail fingertips down his stubbly cheek. "How could I not?"

He smiles at me like I'm the best thing he's ever seen, and I can't stop myself from kissing him again.

Until we hear voices. *Adult* voices.

Grayson and I dart out of our corner, nearly bumping into the others as all of us head for the alcove's opening.

I can't make out the words, but I *do* recognize the sound.

"That's Colleen," I whisper.

"Yeah, and Maurene and Brandon and who knows who else," Eleanor whispers. "We've gotta get out of here and *fast*."

Trembling, I shove my journal into my backpack and shoulder it. We slip cautiously out of the alcove and into the main tunnel.

The floor is basically one big flowstone formation, like giant vats of pancake batter spilled out of the left wall and froze almost instantly. It's slippery and uneven and requires us to lean heavily on the right wall for balance. Our breathing is labored and our hearts hammering, but we can't stop, cannot slow down for an instant. If the others have followed us this far, they're truly determined to have us back.

We reach intersections and always take a quick moment to choose the right path.

Soda straws hang heavily from the low ceiling. We move, hunched and uncomfortable beneath them, smashing our heads and breaking them off every so often. It makes me feel ill every time—not only because we're ruining these beautiful formations, but because we're leaving a trail that the others can follow.

The tunnel makes a sharp twist, widens out, and slopes up. The condensation is practically running water, and when we clamber up the thick flowstone on the far side of this room, it's like climbing into a mouth via a smooth, damp tongue.

Sweat drenches every inch of me. We are hurrying, and hurrying's not safe. My foot slips on the flowstone slope, and I crack my chin, biting my tongue. The thick taste of blood fills my mouth, but I have to ignore it. At the top of the slope, we slide under a narrow ledge, slithering on our bellies until we reach a sheer drop.

We dangle our arms over the edge, glowite extended as far as it can go, but the stones only illuminate a short distance. It's impossible to tell how deep this goes. I lift my arm up to see if we can jump across this chasm, but the other side is all solid rock.

At my feet, the word *LEAP* is scratched.

I glance at Grayson beside me. I know he sees it, too.

"I'll go first," he says.

"Wait," says Eleanor. She drops her glowite onto the floor

below. It shatters, unsurprisingly, but it shows us that we're only maybe fifteen feet up. Very doable.

Grayson wriggles himself around, dropping off the ledge with his arms and then his fingers holding him in place. He takes a deep breath and lets go. He lands ungracefully, but safely.

I go next, mimicking the way he slowly lowered himself, even as my muscles scream in protest. He catches me as I land, arms steadying around my waist. It warms me to my core.

Eleanor follows, and Grayson catches her, too. But when Alice starts to lower herself, she slips, falling sideways. We all reach for her, and slow her fall, but she still lands badly, cracking her head off the stone.

She stays there, limp, on the ground for several terrifying seconds before sitting up and blinking dazedly.

"Alice?" Eleanor whispers, crouched at her side with an arm around her shoulders. "Are you okay?"

Alice rubs her head, grimacing. "I have to be, don't I?" She rises unsteadily to her feet. "I'll be fine. We don't have time to stop."

She definitely has a concussion, and the right thing to do would be to stop, let her rest a little bit, make sure she's fine.

But the problem is, she's right. If we don't keep moving, we're caught. And if we're caught, we're dead.

My mom is the reason I love caves. Hilariously, she hates them. Once, at a rest area, she saw a flyer for Howe Caverns and visibly shuddered. I was seven, so of course immediately interested. I took the flyer and obsessed over it for a full year before the day that my dad looked at my mom and said, "If we don't take her, we'll hear about it for the rest of our lives."

So my mom sucked it up and my parents took us all on a day trip to the touristy but beautiful caverns. From then on, I was hooked.

25

Alice struggles. She carries on without complaint, but stops every so often to throw up, and she stumbles frequently, requiring a lot of support to remain upright and functional. Worry coils heavy in my gut. There's a washed-out look behind her skin. A sunken gloss to her eyes. She falters as we scramble and crouch and edge and crawl over the difficult terrain. We give her extra water to rehydrate her, but still her breaths are raspy and her skin sweaty. None of us knows anything about the proper care of a concussion except don't let her go to sleep. It's extra scary because she was already banged up when we started.

Every time we reach an intersection of tunnels, we search for our three lines. Every time, we choose the tunnel they're drawn beside, and a tiny moment of relief settles into my chest.

But although we haven't heard the sound of their voices in a while, we know that Colleen and the others could be behind us. They could be closing in. I frequently have the type of nightmares where something's chasing me and I try to run but I'm sluggish, can't make my legs speed up enough to outrun it. Where I can feel its hot breath on my back, get that crawling sensation down my spine, where at any moment a claw might reach out and rend me in two.

I feel like that now. My legs are moving but it isn't fast enough. I'm constantly suppressing the urge to glance over my shoulder for a glimpse of what might be lurking in the oppressive blackness.

We keep moving for what feels like about a day; then everyone has to sleep, even Alice. I'm glad we got the rest, because just after we eat what we've decided is breakfast, there's another problem.

Our tunnel narrows to a small opening—a *very* small opening—that we have to crawl through.

We all stand hesitantly before the narrow gap.

"I guess . . . we have to crawl," Alice says uncertainly.

"And what if we don't fit?" Grayson's voice shakes. Honestly, it's a pretty legit question. I'm worried I might not fit, and I'm a wisp comparatively.

"Yeah, pretty sure my hips are not getting through there."

I roll my eyes at Eleanor, whose hips are not at all going to be an issue. She grins, and I realize she was trying to lighten the moment.

"Well," she says, "either we go through or we go back. I'm going through."

And she drops to her stomach, edging into the hole. I admire the way that Eleanor interacts with the world around her. She's so straightforward. Everything is options and you choose the option that feels right to you and go with it.

The rest of us wait like giant chickens, clustered around the low opening.

"It widens out pretty fast!" Eleanor's voice echoes back to us. "But it does get narrower first."

"Narrower." Grayson's voice is pure panic. "I can't fit through narrower."

"Eleanor?" I duck beside the opening. "Can he fit?"

She pauses for too long. "I'm pretty sure."

"Okay." I turn toward Grayson and Alice, trying to appear confident. "I'll go next. Then Grayson, you'll go. That way, if you get a little stuck, we'll have people on either end to help pull you through."

"That works," says Grayson, but he's very pale, and sweating much worse than the rest of us. I place a hand on his arm. "It'll be okay," I promise. "We will get you through no matter what."

I take a moment to gather myself, almost uncontrollably anxious about getting my own body through. Eleanor is taller than me, but is she wider? My stomach kneads itself until I want to throw up, but I put on a brave face. I still love caves. This is an adventure.

If only it wasn't the life-or-death kind.

You can do this, Eliza, I repeat over and over in my head. I have to get through this because I cannot be the one who gets stuck. I will not. I take a deep breath and lower myself to the ground. The faint light of glowite emanates from the other end of the tunnel. *Breathe.*

Pushing my backpack ahead, I ease into the crevice. It narrows quickly, flattening me out entirely. I can't lift my head at all without bumping it on jagged rock, and every time I breathe, I fear that the expansion of my lungs will make me too big for the space. Inch by inch, I creep through the narrowest part, but I cannot relax until I've reached Eleanor. The ceiling is still low here, but the walls are wider, and we crouch side by side with no problem. Eleanor's eyes meet mine, mirroring my worry. I *barely* squeezed through, and now Grayson has to try it.

He's broad-shouldered, and if he hadn't lost bulk due to our never-quite-enough diet, he wouldn't stand a chance. As it is . . .

I gnaw ferociously on a fingernail.

The ragged sound of Grayson's breathing edges closer as he attempts the passage. And then . . . it stops moving closer.

"You okay?" I call out.

Silence. Then: "I'm stuck."

"You're okay," Eleanor says immediately. "You're not stuck; you just *feel* stuck. Eliza and I will pull on your arms and help get you through."

"No, Eleanor, I'm *really* stuck. My shoulders are too wide. I can't—can't go forward and I can't go back I'm *trapped* I can't move I—"

"You have to calm down," says Alice, her voice muffled. "I'm coming behind you. I'll push on your feet while the others pull on your arms."

"I can't do it." Grayson is sobbing, I realize, and the sound pulls a lump to my throat.

My jaw clenches tight as I turn to Eleanor. "We're getting him out of there. We're not going anywhere without him."

"Of course not," says Eleanor. "If you crawl in a little bit, you'll be able to grab on to his arms. And then I'll pull your feet. Sound like a plan?"

"Yes." I take a deep breath and crawl back into the tunnel. I slip my hands into Grayson's outstretched, sweat-slicked palms. "You have to hold on to me really tight, okay?"

"Okay," he whispers.

"Ready?"

Silence.

"Grayson?"

"Yeah, I'm—Eliza, I'm really scared."

I squeeze his hands tight. "I know. But we're not going to leave you. I promise. I—we need you. We're not leaving you here."

"Okay. I'm ready."

He says that part loudly enough so everyone can hear, and Eleanor's fists tighten around my ankles.

"You're going to have to pull harder than that!" I shout.

"Don't want to hurt you," Eleanor replies.

"I'm fine. Just *pull*."

She yanks harder, and stone scrapes roughly against my stomach as I'm stretched back. The muscles in my shoulders wail in pain, but whatever pain I'm feeling, Grayson is getting it tenfold. Alice pushing on his feet, Eleanor and me yanking on his arms. He screams and I feel hesitation from Eleanor, so I yell at her not to stop. Grayson is moving. Slowly, painfully, but he's moving.

Tears sting my eyes and I bite down on my lip until it splits to stop myself from crying out, because my arms feel ready to break free from their sockets. It hurts, it *hurts*, but Grayson needs my help and I can't give up now.

I feel like an ant holding on to an earthworm, being yanked from the ground by a bird. Grayson's screams have reduced to whimpers, his breaths shuddery and pained. And then, without warning, he shouts, "I'm free! You can stop."

Eleanor instantly lets go of my legs. I don't let go of Grayson's hands.

"You sure?" I ask.

"Yeah." He grimaces. "My hips are just about through that narrowest part. I think I can pull myself the rest of the way now."

I back off, and he does manage, dragging himself out like a beached merman. His shirt is bloodied and torn. He winces with every movement, and I feel awful.

"Grayson, I'm so sorry," I say as Alice emerges from the tunnel in his wake. "I had no idea this would—"

"You shouldn't be apologizing." He waves it away, and winces again. "You got me through, just like you promised. I—thank you."

I smile at him. "You're welcome."

After we've finished tending to his wounds the best we can, Grayson catches my chin between his fingers. It steals my breath and I'm suddenly keenly aware of the fact that we were kissing in the not-so-distant past. "You're bleeding, too," he says.

"Oh. Yeah." I dab at my lip with a finger. "I just—it hurt, that's all, but I was trying to be strong. I shouldn't have bitten down so hard."

"You should have said it hurt too much."

"I'm okay. I'm fine. We needed to get you out, and we couldn't exactly stop in the middle of the process."

His eyes narrow. "Yes, we could."

I roll my shoulders. Very sore. But I'll live. "Well, it's over. I'm fine, you're going to be fine, we all made it. Everything's good."

It's lies, and he knows it. That's the second time he's been injured by a narrow passage, and we've got *days* ahead of us, if not longer. We could be in very serious trouble here, much as I don't want to admit it. Or think about it.

I've been pushing it away. The fear that we might not make it. That Colleen was right and this is not leading us anywhere except our graves. But now it envelops me, clinging to the thick cavern air. I can't escape it.

I may not be able to escape at *all*.

There's a pretty well-known horror manga that I can't stop thinking about right now. The story features these person-shaped holes that appeared in a mountainside. People are finding holes shaped exactly like themselves and being compelled into them, they just can't stop themselves. Once they're inside, they can't go backward. The holes eventually stretch and twist, distorting their bodies because they have to keep moving forward. The story ends with formless fissures being discovered on the other side of the mountain, and the discoverers realizing that something—the distorted form of the people who entered on the other side—is coming toward them from inside the fissure.

I've never been one for claustrophobia, but...I think I'm starting to be.

26

"It's getting warmer," I say. This has been bugging me for a while. The air feels *different* but I couldn't place why. Now, though, I'm confident that it's temperature.

"That's kind of expected, though, right?" says Alice. She's doing much better after a good long rest we took, and it's a huge relief.

I shrug. "I mean, yeah. It should be much worse, though."

And it could *get* much worse, but I'm not gonna say that to Alice.

"Better warm than cold, right?" says Eleanor.

I smile at her. "Since we don't have unlimited clothing at our disposal, I'd say so, yeah."

Grayson, in the front of the group, stops abruptly. He holds up a fist, the signal we decided upon to mean *be silent*, and my heart whirs like an overworked engine.

In the dim-lit silence, my hearing sharpens. Catches a squelching noise somewhere ahead. I slip out my knife, watching the others do the same, and then Grayson moves a tiny shift, and I see . . . *it.*

The creature is translucent white, like a grub. I can easily trace its nervous system and its digestive tract down the length of its body, dark strips that end near a cluster of reproductive organs at its rear. It has a single eye in the center of its forehead, and from time to time it pulls a clear membrane over the eye and back up. The eye is pale and cloudy, and it's unclear whether it is functional or for decoration. Down here, sight isn't the most necessary of senses.

Its mouth is a horror show. Teeth like knives, about an inch wide at their base, and tapering into sharp points after roughly four inches of length. And there are too many. The teeth are crammed together in a circular shape, jutting out in front of peeled-back lips that clearly cannot contain this mouth.

But it has no limbs, no other weapons.

None of us has moved, and neither has it. Grayson pulls out an arrow, and slowly, carefully notches it into his bow. He aims for that gaping mouth, and when he fires, the arrow shoots true, lodging itself in the thing's throat.

It flails, letting out a guttural hiss. Chomps its teeth down, breaking off the end of the arrow. It's dying, but it's not dead, and it intends to take at least one of us with it.

I move my knife, but Eleanor is faster. She lodges her weapon deep into its general throat area, just as it lunges for her, raking its sharp teeth over her shoulder. She howls, slumps to the floor.

The rest of us close in on the creature. I stab it in the side, and when my fist touches its sticky flesh, it burns.

A low curse word from Grayson, beside me, tells me I'm not the only one who's discovered this. But we stab and stab and stab anyway, until the creature is dead and oozing on the floor.

I ignore the throbbing, burning pain in my fist and hurry to Eleanor's side. She's gasping and clutching her neck.

That's when I realize, with horror, that its teeth didn't just sink into her shoulder.

"Let's patch you up." I try to keep my voice calm, but I'm not. I'm not. When she takes her hand away, I don't know what I'll see and she's suddenly so pale.

She opens her mouth and a sound like drowning comes out. *No.*

"You're going to be fine," I tell her, sweeping hair out of her eyes. "We can't do this without you, so you're going to be—"

She shakes her head, almost imperceptibly, and squeezes her eyes shut, pained.

Alice is at my shoulder. "I've got the bandages and stuff," she says breathlessly. "What . . ."

She trails off because, like me, she's noticed the way Eleanor clutches at her neck, the way that blood seeps through her fingers, and the way her breaths rattle through her throat.

"Let's get this bleeding stopped," I say desperately. And then, to Eleanor, "We love you. We're going to fix you."

Alice nods.

Eleanor mouths something, but I can't make out the word.

I lean closer and in the undertones of her rattling breath, I hear, *"Dying."*

"No," I say placatingly, ignoring the chill that washes over my whole body. "You're okay. You're going to be fine."

Her eyelids flutter, and her hand slips away from the wound on her neck. The unfixable, awful wound. Blood glugs thickly out the side of her neck, pooling behind her head. She's been unsavable since the moment those teeth sank into her flesh.

And now she's gone.

"No," I whisper. A numbness spreads through my body. I'm too shocked to cry; instead, I panic. Press my hand over the wound even though it stops nothing, even though there's already too much blood on the floor and not enough inside of her. "You can't—you have to, you wanted to go *home*. You're supposed to make it home."

Now I'm weeping. My face is coated in tears, and when I go to wipe them away, they're replaced with a hot smear of blood.

I clench a fist into her shirt. "Come *back*," I order.

A hand presses against my shoulder blades, and I snap to awareness. "You have to let go," Grayson says gently, and I don't know if he means physically or emotionally.

I pull my hand away, bury my face in my knees, and sob so hard, it feels like all my organs might float away. Grayson wraps both arms around me, holding tight. I clutch at him and absorb what comfort I can, which isn't much.

Eleanor and I were supposed to make it. *Together.* She's the best person I've ever known. So wonderful and funny and sweet.

She pushed me, not in the way that Sherri used to push me, but in a way that got me outside my comfort zone and made me okay with it. She had family, friends. They would have been so excited to see her again, and now—

Now, I wonder, what if *none* of us make it? What if Colleen was right and this was a suicidal idea and we should have just resigned ourselves to life in this cavern, stayed here forever?

No. *No.* Eleanor would not have wanted me thinking like this. I have to pull it together. We have to keep going.

"We shouldn't have left."

Those words have been sloshing around in the back of my skull, but now I'm hearing them aloud. From Alice's mouth. I look at her through tear-blurred eyes. Her mouth and brow are pinched.

"We had to," Grayson says.

"We *didn't*, though." Her voice rises. "Eliza and I got this dangerous idea in our heads, and it was the *worst* idea. Eleanor would be alive right now if we hadn't left that cavern."

Each word is a kick to the ribs. The last sentence cracks them, and I can't breathe.

That's when I do something foolish: I grab my glowite, and I flee.

Not far, just until I'm a bit farther down the tunnel, past the corpse of the insect larva, and out of sight of the others. I still can't really breathe and I can hear the two of them arguing.

This is my fault.

It's *all* my fault.

Eleanor trusted me, she *trusted* me, and I was not smart enough or strong enough to get her through this to safety. I have to be strong enough now, but how can I do that without her?

I think about what Eleanor said, how she told me I'm brave, but she's *wrong*. I'm not brave. I'm impulsive. Something I never thought was true, but see all too clearly now.

I haven't learned a single freaking thing from all the times I've messed up. All the things I've agreed to that were foolish. Now *I'm* the Sherri, and it cost the life of someone who deserves to be here much more than I do.

Footsteps echo from farther down the tunnel, and I feel a new emotion: fear. I wield my glowite and my knife, but it's only Grayson. He plucks both weapons from my grip, sets them against the wall, and then hugs me tight, kissing my hair.

"Alice is just upset. Upset and feeling guilty, same as you, though neither of you are remotely to blame."

"I've never . . ." I pause to wipe roughly at my cheeks. They're swollen and puffy from the crying, and also from whatever venom is on that larva's skin, rubbed from my hand to my face and making me itchy and achy. "I've never lost anyone close to me before. I mean, my gramp, but he was eighty-six and died peacefully in his sleep. No one *young*, or no one—what if this *is* my fault? It feels like my fault, Grayson."

He cups my face in both hands, frowning at me. "If it's your fault, then it's mine, too, and Alice's. We're in this together. We decided to do this *together*. You can't take the blame, you don't deserve to. It's too heavy a burden, and it's not fair or right. We all knew this was dangerous. Eleanor included."

I bury my face in his chest and say nothing.

After a few minutes, he says quietly, "My dad died when I was eleven. Car accident, and he'd been drinking. I was with him."

I look up at him, horrified.

"He blew past a yield sign without even looking. A car was coming, and smashed full-on into the side of our truck. My dad was killed pretty much instantly. The woman driving the other car almost didn't make it. They had to amputate her arm, and she had a traumatic brain injury. I had some broken bones, but they all healed." His eyes flick away from mine, to the wall behind me. "I—for a really long time, I blamed myself for what happened to my dad, and to that woman. I knew he was in no condition to drive. My parents were divorced and it was because my dad couldn't—well, he could be pretty rough. My mom had given me a secret cell phone to call her if I ever felt unsafe. I should have used it then; I *knew* I should have. But I didn't and he died and that other woman's life is completely destroyed, and I thought that was my fault."

"But you were eleven," I protest. "He was a grown man who decided to drive drunk."

He nods. "Exactly. I understand that now. We're all responsible for the decisions we make. We knew, we *all knew* that this was a dangerous plan. But don't forget, there was a danger to staying behind, too. The bioluminescents, and the way Colleen acted when you said you were leaving . . . That cavern, it's an illusion of safety. We haven't been safe since the moment we set foot in this place. Eleanor knew that and I'm—" He stops, swallows hard. His voice is scratchier when he continues. "I'm going to miss her so much, but she would not have wanted you to blame yourself for this. She would have wanted you to stay strong and lead us out of here."

I rise onto my toes and kiss him. Gently at first, and then more desperately. "You need to stay with me," I tell him. "You have to make it out of here with me. I can't lose you and Eleanor both, I just can't."

He kisses me back, fiercely. "Same to you."

I start to cry again then, and I can't stop. I lose all the strength in my body, collapse to the floor.

Grayson doesn't say anything. He just sits beside me and holds my hand.

Eleanor has only been part of my life for, like, less than 2% of it. But I already don't know what to do without her here. Why did she have to die? Of all of us, why her? We left so that we could live.

Eleanor just really deserved to live.

27

When we return to Alice, little has changed. All three of us remain heartbroken. Eleanor remains a still, lifeless form on the ground. The only real difference is that the pool of blood on the floor has grown, forming a dark halo around Eleanor's head. I feel sick.

"What . . . happens next?" Grayson asks.

Alice stands, slowly. "Well, we have to go on. We don't have any other choice."

"But what do we do . . ." Grayson swallows hard. ". . . with Eleanor?"

"We'll have to just . . . make this a good resting place for her." My mouth trembles. No part of me wants to leave her here, but we can't drag her around, either. It'd be undignified.

Alice helps me wrap Eleanor's neck in gauze and otherwise clean up her body as best we can. Grayson keeps watch for insects or anything else that might want to kill us. The three of us take a moment to stand over Eleanor and say goodbye in our own silent ways. My mind feels numb. The ache of loss is so deep there's a physical pain in my chest.

But we have to go on, because if we don't, if we stop and give up, then everything we've done would have been in vain and Eleanor would have died for nothing,

The passages ahead are narrow and steep. And, because it's just our luck, before long we find ourselves in a spot where the only exit is a low-ceilinged tunnel. We're going to have to crawl on our bellies. Again.

"Oh great." Grayson folds his arms.

The tunnel makes me feel like I'm going to have a panic attack, so I throw myself into it first. That way, if something goes wrong, I won't be surrounded on two sides with other people.

Of course, if the thing that goes wrong is that the tunnel ends, I'll be trapped between rock and a person, but that doesn't occur to me until I'm already edging along, barely breathing.

You are not going to die, Eliza. You are not *going to die.*

I scream it over and over in my mind because if I don't, I can't keep going. My muscles ache with the effort and my brain is begging me to give up and rest for a while.

The tunnel seems never-ending. And the farther I get, the smaller it feels, even though there's actually, thankfully, plenty of space. I only hope Grayson isn't struggling to fit.

Finally, I emerge onto a thin ledge. I'd put my glowite into my backpack before starting to crawl, and now I can't see a thing. The next person out is Alice, and she brings light.

I really . . . *really* wish she hadn't.

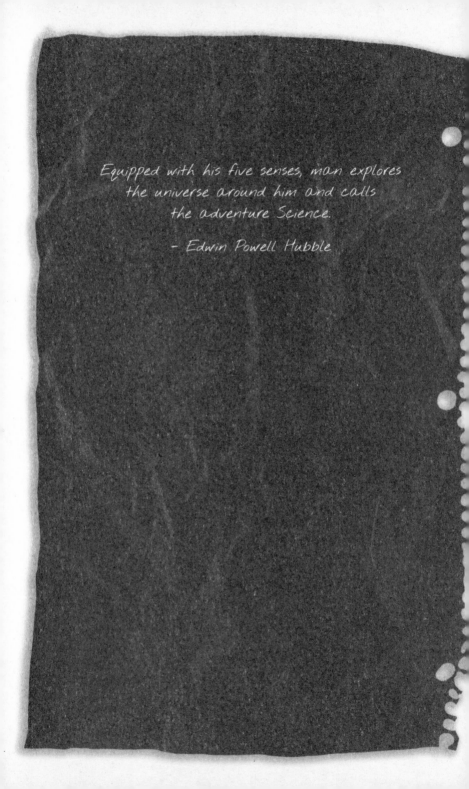

Equipped with his five senses, man explores
the universe around him and calls
the adventure Science.

— Edwin Powell Hubble

28

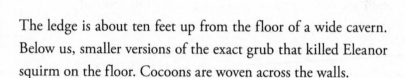

The ledge is about ten feet up from the floor of a wide cavern. Below us, smaller versions of the exact grub that killed Eleanor squirm on the floor. Cocoons are woven across the walls.

"Eliza." Alice's voice is sheer terror.

"I know." I edge back, pressing myself as close to the wall as possible. There are two tunnels branching off the room, but to get to either, we have to get past these . . . monsters. I can't see any markings, either. Not from up here.

Grayson squeezes out of the tunnel and sucks in a breath.

"If we had something to distract them with," he whispers, "just long enough that we could get past . . ."

"What, though?" Alice asks.

"I don't know. Food?"

"Um." I think of something. Something terrible. Something that makes me want to rip out my own brain to remove the thought. Something that might be our only option. "Eleanor might . . . be of help here."

"That's . . . I don't know, Eliza." Alice grimaces. The grubs below continue clicking their horrid jaws, oozing around in their filthy nest.

"It's awful, I know it is." I fold my arms tight. My fingertips tingle with anxiety. "But I think she would want to help us."

"I'll go back and get her," Grayson says quietly. "That tunnel wasn't *so* tight. I could figure out how to pull her through it."

"You don't—"

"Just stay here, and stay quiet. I'll be back soon, and if you hear me yell, then just . . . I don't know, run, I guess."

He leaves with a squeeze of my hand, and then Alice and I wait in an agonized silence for him to return.

"Do you wish it was me who died?" Alice whispers, when the silence grows too heavy. "Instead of Eleanor?"

"I would *never* wish that. Why would I wish that?"

Alice shrugs, looks away. "I'm older. We're not as close. I just . . . I don't know. Feel like it should have been me."

"It shouldn't have been any of us." I frown. "And you're not that much older."

She nods, gives me a weak, apologetic smile. "Sorry. Just being insecure, I guess."

"I know a thing or two about insecurity." I edge slightly closer and reach for her hand, squeeze it tight. She brushes a tear from her cheek. Comforting others, usually it's my wheelhouse. It's the thing I do that doesn't make me feel socially awkward or anxious. But right now, I don't know what to say. This isn't like commiserating with Meg because her mom's being a jerk again. Or because she probably didn't do well on that math test or the boy she's maybe starting to like flirted with some other girl. Meg has always been easy, because all she wanted was the attention and the comfort. I could do that no problem.

What Alice is feeling, that cannot be fixed. Not with a squeeze of my hand, not with an arm around her waist or a head against her shoulder. Not with any words that exist. Not with anything except maybe time. And maybe . . . maybe sunlight.

I wonder if I'll be able to face the sun, though. After this.

It isn't long before Grayson returns, I don't think, but it feels eternal.

Seeing Eleanor's limp form, my stomach turns into a nest of snakes. I don't feel good about this at all now. We edge as far to the right as we can on this outcropping, and choose the closest tunnel by default. Even though this was my idea, I shut my eyes when Grayson heaves Eleanor's body over the edge, as close to the middle of the cavern as he can get. My gut lurches when I hear the awful, squelching sound of the landing, but I open my eyes to jump down.

And flat out sprint. We don't know how fast these things are, but hopefully not fast enough that they'll go after us when they have easy prey.

We meet two of them in the tunnel. Alice takes care of one, and I sink my knife deep into the other. And we continue on. It's a wide tunnel, so we're able to bunch together, running as fast as we can.

We barrel through caverns, choosing tunnels at random; anything that seems to head deeper into the earth.

The thing that finally brings us to a stop again is a river. It's in a medium-sized cavern filled with beautiful cave formations, like nothing we've ever seen. And it *glitters* with bioluminescence. This cavern is *alive*. So breathtaking, I choke back tears.

We walk through slowly, awestricken, surrounded by glowing colors. The ceiling is maybe ten feet high, and illuminated by dangling plants like the one in my backpack. Only these are electric pink. I reach up a hand and brush my fingertips along their delicate ends. They rustle, like feathery seaweed.

Glowite is everywhere, and in a myriad of colors—red, blue, green, purple. All the formations are lit up like museum exhibits. Luminous orange, purple, and yellow mushrooms grow in clusters along the floor and some of the formations. Water moves sluggishly along the far edge of the room, and even that glows. Tiny, glittering creatures swirl beneath the surface, all the way down to the stony bottom. Steam rises in lazy coils above the surface. I crouch beside the water and cautiously submerge a finger. It's quite warm. Almost uncomfortably warm, like a hot tub.

Alice joins me. "Warm?" she asks.

"Hot."

She tests it. "Oh wow."

I pull my knees to my chest. "Eleanor would have really loved to see this."

Alice skims her fingers along the water's surface. "She would."

I watch her silently for a few minutes while Grayson circles the cavern, checking out all the formations. I think we've come to the unspoken agreement that we'll be spending the night here. It'd be pretty tough, at least, for something to sneak up on us in this place. Maybe that's why, while it's completely teeming with life, none of that life is predatory.

"What made you decide to leave?" I ask. "I mean, I know it was my journal and it was your injury, but, like, what *really* made you decide it?"

I hope my question doesn't sound like total nonsense. Prying makes me so anxious, but I've known Alice as long as anyone else, yet I don't *know* her the way I know Grayson, the way I knew Eleanor. I know she's twenty-three and that she'd been almost finished with a degree in business. She ended up here when she got separated from friends during a spelunking adventure about a year ago. But that's it. I don't know anything about her history or her interests or what she was planning to do for work. Who she left behind, who she doesn't miss. She's been somewhat of a closed book.

"It woke me up," she says. "I don't *belong* here. No offense because I know you're, like, totally into caves and stuff, but this . . . I only went spelunking the first time because my friends said it was ridiculously good exercise. I kept doing it because they were right. The caves themselves, I don't care for at all. It was part of the adrenaline of the thing, you know? I hated the feeling of it; I hated the dark spaces and the tiny crevices. But afterward I would feel so *alive*, when I came back into the world and the sun was hot on my face and my muscles were tired. This is just . . . it's the world's longest spelunking adventure and I'm ready to be done. I'm supposed to be starting my life as an adult. Not camping out and waiting to die."

"So you'll probably never step foot in a cave again after this, huh?"

She laughs. "You *will*?"

I shrug. "I mean, probably. Just . . . carefully."

She laughs again. "Good for you, I guess. I, on the other hand, will be sticking firmly to aboveground terrain. I don't even want to go into a basement after this."

"Watch. You'll end up missing it."

"The day that happens, I'm scheduling myself immediately for therapy."

We're *all* going to need therapy after this, I think. Or, in my case, *extra* therapy. I cannot begin to fathom how I'm going to process what's happened to me when I get back into the real world.

If, my brain whispers. I ignore it, but it gets louder: *Eleanor thought she'd make it back to the real world, too. Just because you believe in something doesn't mean it's possible.*

I press fingers to my temples, trying to squeeze the thoughts out. Shaken by my abrupt loss, I'm starting to have a very hard time with my confidence. Who decided I was right? Who decided that I had any ability at all to decide something like this, be responsible for the welfare of others? I can barely manage to be responsible for myself.

I heave a large sigh, trying to calm my racing heart.

"You okay?" Alice asks.

"Yeah." I stand up. "Just tired."

Exhausted, more like. Drained to my very bones.

Our new debate: whether we should try eating the mushrooms. Grayson and I are not on the same team.

I know *everything* glows down here, but to me, a radioactive-orange mushroom screams, *DO NOT EAT ME,* and I cannot believe it doesn't scream this to everyone.

"Are you *trying* to die?" I ask, snatching away a mushroom that Grayson picked.

"No," he says irritably. "I'm trying to *eat*. If these mushrooms are edible, wouldn't that be so much easier than trying to kill insects for food? These mushrooms look like glowing versions of a morel. Edible, and tasty."

"Aren't there poisonous lookalikes to that?" I ask.

Grayson sighs. "There are poisonous lookalikes to most mushrooms. But I feel really confident about this."

"If he wants to eat it, let him," says Alice. "He's the one who'll suffer if he's wrong."

"You mean he's the one who will *die*," I snap.

"We're all gonna die of something," Alice mutters.

If Eleanor were here, she'd say something to cheer us all up. But she's not.

"Whatever," I say. "Just make sure you cook it thoroughly."

"I will," Grayson says to my retreating back.

Annoyance flares in my chest. He *promised* he wouldn't die. He said he would get out of here with me. And yet he's stubbornly refusing to see why eating a glowing mushroom might be an incredibly dumb idea.

I don't watch. I sit by myself at the water's edge, and I don't care if it makes me look petulant. Neither of them comes to sit with me, and I don't care about that, either. Alice can come get me when Grayson's dying in a frothing heap on the floor, or when it's been long enough that we know he'll be okay. Until then, I welcome the solitude.

Alice does, eventually, approach me. "He's fine," she says. "Guess the mushrooms aren't poisonous."

"Cool. Thanks."

She doesn't leave, so I look up at her. Her arms are folded, and her posture stiff.

"It bothered you, didn't it? What I said before about death."

I just shrug.

"I shouldn't have been so flippant." She sits. "I'm just . . . We all process in our own ways, you know? Everything feels different without her. It all feels wrong."

"Yeah." Tears well up in my eyes. "It does feel wrong. It feels like I led us into this and I let us all down, Eleanor most of all. And I'm not even—I'm not a leader at all. I don't know why everyone thinks, somehow, that I'm capable."

"You are, though. Maybe you don't want to be. Maybe it doesn't fit naturally. But it is what it is. You agreed to lead us in this, whether you meant to or not, and it's a little late to back out now."

It's not what I wanted to hear, but maybe it's what I needed to hear. Pouting at the side of an underground river isn't a great way to deal with my emotions. Maybe I need to swallow down all the bad feelings for right now, and deal with them later. When I'm out. When I'm *home*.

I run fingers through my greasy hair. "It scares me to let people down," I confess.

Alice purses her lips. "I think you'll find that most people don't love letting others down."

"No chance that mushroom kills Grayson?"

Alice shrugs. "Seems unlikely."

"Okay. I guess I should go back over, then."

"There you go." She smiles.

I return the smile, waveringly, and trudge back to where we've set up camp. Grayson's roasting mushrooms over a fire built from detritus and lit by his lighter. He looks up at me with a hint of guilt in his eyes, and it makes me feel bad. Testing an unfamiliar mushroom was dangerous, but I didn't react the way I should have, either.

I sit cross-legged beside him and lean my head on his shoulder. "Thanks for not dying."

"I wouldn't have tried it if I wasn't confident." He kisses my hair and slips his hand into mine. "I promised we'd live through this together, and I'm not gonna forget."

Later, I try the mushrooms, and they're surprisingly tasty. After weeks of insects and algae, my mouth is ready for a different flavor. Between the edible mushrooms and the beauty of this cavern, our spirits rise ever so slightly.

I should enjoy not having to be in charge all the time—it's nice, actually, that Grayson and Alice found us a new food.

If only Eleanor were here to share it, too.

29

After the beautiful cavern, we begin to see glowing things more often. Glowite, particularly. Lodged sporadically into the walls of tunnels. We barely need our lights, which is nice except that the brightness makes me feel exposed.

But the brief respite we experienced in that beautiful place is not, it seems, to be re-created. The air is muggy and uncomfortable. We wear a layer of sweat full-time, like an undergarment. The sweat stings in the cuts all over my body. The mugginess feels like, as Alice puts it, a dog's mouth.

The tunnels are slippery and dripping, clogged with flowstones and stalactites. Creatures, too. Some glowing, some not. Most, trying to eat us.

Today, we've stumbled upon a nest of something like what killed Eleanor, only much, much smaller. They lunge at us with their too-toothy jaws and actually spit the substance they secrete that causes burning and itchiness.

But we slaughter them. Mercilessly. Brutally. This is our

revenge, and each time my knife plunges into one of those gooey bodies, it gives my heart a brief moment of peace.

Even if, after, we're all sore and wincing from our burn wounds.

"Does this look right to you, Eliza?" Grayson asks me, crouched beside one tunnel.

It has the three lines, but fainter than usual. And something else, near the floor. I brush aside debris. "It says *CAUTION* right here."

Alice crouches to look. "Huh. Wonder why here and nowhere else?"

"Because it's getting more dangerous," says Grayson. "The deeper we go, the more trouble we're in."

"That's not . . ." I trail off because he isn't entirely wrong, unfortunately. Tension between the three of us has been increasing as the heat and the danger and the pain has made us irritable. Soon, it's going to snap.

"I'm worried about this," Grayson says.

"Why?" Alice folds her arms. "What's more worrying now than before?"

Grayson laughs, harshly. "I don't know, Alice. Think what we've been through already, and that *didn't* warrant use of the word *caution*."

"Well, we can't exactly go back," I point out.

"I know." Grayson runs fingers through his hair. "I'm just . . . I want to be done. I want this to be over."

"We all want this to be *over*." Alice leans against the wall. "This is miserable. I miss—I miss the colony."

My stomach knots anxiously. "But not as much as you miss home, right?"

Alice glances up at me with a frown. "Right." It's unconvincing. "Anyway, we can't go back, so let's go on."

We do, but we're all quiet and miserable and I'm quite sure that they're both blaming me for this, seething about me in the silence. It gnaws at me, sends tingling numbness up my arms.

"I'm sorry I caused this," I tell them, when I can't stand it anymore.

Alice, in front, stops. Her foot rests on a broken-off chunk of stalagmite.

"You know," she says with a heavy sigh, "there's something I didn't say to you about reading your journal. Mainly because I knew reading it wasn't cool in the first place."

I clutch involuntarily at the straps of my backpack even though that ship has long since sailed. "And what's that?"

"Your friends truly suck."

It's the last thing I expected her to say, and I can't help the laughter that escapes my lips. Alice laughs, too.

"No, but I'm serious," she insists. "You are a kind, smart person, Eliza. You have so much to offer, and yet for some reason you don't seem able to believe that you're worth anything."

My stomach clenches. "You're right. I do have trouble with that. I have trouble . . . with people in general. If you knew how much of my life was spent recapping conversations in my head and picking them apart for all the ways I embarrassed myself, you'd be appalled. I'd like to blame it on my friends, but . . . that's all internal."

"Sure," says Grayson. "And there's nothing you can really do about that, right? It's just how your brain works. But what you *can* do is stop wasting any energy on people who make that feeling worse instead of making it better. Alice and I aren't mad at you. You didn't cause this. The situation's frustrating and we're tired and we want to be safe again, but you woke us up, Eliza. This cave is a parasite and it wormed inside our brains and made us think the colony was where we belonged. You freed us."

A lump forms in my throat. "That makes me sound, like, a thousand percent more heroic than I ever could dream to be."

Grayson grins at me in a way that makes my heart loosen in my chest. "Well, I'm not taking it back."

I stare at him for a long moment. Marveling that, somehow, this person I've barely known for any time at all cares so much about me. That he's *kissed* me and that I know he'll do it again.

"Okay, as the third wheel here, this is getting a touch awkward," says Alice, poking at my shoulder with a finger.

"Sorry." I turn back around. "Let's keep going. And I'll try to stop apologizing so much. Even though I just did it again."

Alice laughs. "We'll start you with a clean slate, right now."

"Yeah, and—" Grayson is cut off by a loud, urgent *shh* by Alice.

"I heard something," she whispers.

Instantly, we're all on alert. Silent. I hear nothing. And I can tell by the others' expressions that neither do they.

"Maybe it was nothing," Alice whispers again, uncertain. "Maybe—"

Something leaps out from the shadows ahead and grabs her roughly by the arms. Before I have even registered what it is, cold hands grip my wrists, holding them tight behind my back. Wrapping something around them.

Bioluminescents.

They've found us, and they're tying us up.

I scream. It's long and loud, filled with all the pain and fear possessed in my heart.

I wanted to make it. I really, deep down inside, thought we would make it. But it turns out that Colleen was right after all. We should never have left.

And we're going to pay for the mistake with our lives.

Everyone has heard of Marie Curie. Everyone knows she was the first woman to win a Nobel Prize and that she researched radioactivity. And everyone also knows that her very important scientific work is also what killed her. Sometimes, scientists die in the pursuit of new info. We're a curious bunch. Book-smart but not always street-smart. I think Mary's very aware of this, maybe too aware. And maybe that's why she didn't leave with us. All her geological discoveries down here, she'd trade her life for them. And I don't know if it's good or bad that I don't feel the same way.

30

I don't know what they did to knock us out. I have no memory of it happening. But all three of us wake almost simultaneously, groaning and struggling. We're tied to a post in the middle of a spacious cavern. It's dazzling. Even with the danger of the current situation looming over me, I can't help taking a moment to admire it all.

Everything in here glows, like so many of the tunnels and caverns since that first glowing cavern we came across. But it's more . . . organized. The plants dangling from the ceiling have been woven together, forming tapestries of color and patterns that mean nothing to me but probably a lot to these people. Mushrooms grow in a cultivated manner across one side of the cavern, and behind a tightly woven fence, insects mill about, chirping and rustling. These are different than any we've seen. They look like long-legged, wingless dragonflies and they have luminescent blue stripes down their backs.

Pathways are etched out by rows of glowite, and

bioluminescent humans move in and out of tunnels, most shoot-ing us furtive glances. None making direct eye contact.

My heart pounds so hard I feel faint. I tug in vain on my binds, but I'm tied up securely.

Then three bioluminescents walk right up to us, observ-ing us like we're livestock at an auction. They don't speak ver-bally, but I immediately recognize their language of gestures and motions. Of course, I don't know enough to catch most of it.

I stare, mesmerized by their glow, by the way their organs and muscles and veins shift inside their bodies as they move. Their facial expressions change as their gestured conversation continues, and fear wells up inside me. With fingernails more like claws, they could hurt me easily. One licks his lips and I get a glimpse of canine-like teeth. Sharp and menacing.

After some more gesturing, they come even closer. One plucks at the skin on Alice's arm, and then does the same to mine. They start gesturing again, and I think they're talking about the different shades of our skin.

Are they going to eat us? I speculate. They might not see us as the same species. They might not think of it as cannibalism.

Or they might not care.

Maybe they wonder if there's a taste difference between darker and lighter flesh. Maybe we look delicious compared to the limited selection they're presented with regularly.

I'm spiraling into the kind of panic I usually reserve for

overwhelming social situations. My limbs have gone numb and I can't tell if my heart is racing or not beating at all.

The bioluminescents move away from Alice and me, observing the stubble on Grayson's cheeks and tugging at the edges of his clothing. One starts plucking at my clothing, too, and I hold my breath. They're not trying to *remove* our clothing, far as I can tell. They just seem baffled by it.

They're all fully naked. This warm, humid environment probably doesn't lend itself to anyone deciding they have a need for clothing. I'm sure life's easier if you don't care about things like that.

The silence gets to me. The way they make absolutely no sound even when I'm pretty sure they're laughing. Sharp teeth bared and neck thrown back, eyes crinkled with delight. The accompanying silence itches my skin. It's like looking at a face-swap photo. Everything seems kinda regular but something is just skin-crawlingly *wrong* about it.

To stop myself from thinking about what it will feel like to be eaten, I think about the bioluminescent woman who gave me my glowing plant. The peace offering, according to Mary.

My eyes sweep over the room, over the glowing plants on the ceiling and the floor. Actually, none of them are purple, like my plant. Have I seen any purple ones at all? I crane my neck, trying to see every corner of this cavern.

There. I catch a tiny glimpse of purple. It's in one of the pens, just a tiny patch, carefully cultivated.

It's not common, my plant, the peace offering. If we hadn't

attacked her, the gesture might have been successful. And now . . .
now I could try the same tactic. What do I have to lose?

I point with my toe to my backpack, wiggling my foot
until they notice. One of them finally does, and cautiously
approaches the backpack. I nod eagerly, hoping that means the
same thing to them, or that it at least doesn't mean something
bad. If I had my hands, I could speak to them, at least explain
the basics. That we're not here to hurt them.

The man fumbles with the zipper, startling when he tugs on
it and it slides. Then he's distracted, sliding it back a few times
and gesturing with obvious amusement for the other two to try
it as well. I swallow my impatience. This *has* to work.

Finally, he opens the backpack and brings it to me. He
frees my hands from their binds but holds a knifelike object
toward me in an obvious gesture of threat. Moving slowly, I
crouch before the backpack, rummage through until I find my
plant.

It's harder than I expected to give it up. This plant, somehow,
has become a source of comfort to me. But I hold it out in front of
me, fingers trembling. I make eye contact and I don't break it.

The nearest bioluminescent man's mouth falls open, his
eyes widen. And then . . . he looks angry. Their gesturing
becomes faster, harsher in motion. I catch a few things, like
stolen and *must have killed one of us*.

"No!" I say aloud, and then I gesture the same thing, which
only seems to anger them more.

They tie me back up, and one presses a knife to my throat.

Grayson makes a small sound, but I can tell he and Alice both are trying to stay quiet so as not to anger them further.

How do you know our language? another asks, gesturing slowly. Of course, I can't answer.

But I don't have to, because suddenly, Mary's here.

Mary is here.

She gestures wildly and frantically at the two who *aren't* holding knives to my throat. Her back is to me, so I can't tell what she's saying. And the bioluminescents' expressions are utterly still, so I don't know how they're taking it.

After what feels like an eternity, they all seem to come to an understanding, and the knife leaves my throat. I swallow hard, trying not to imagine what might have happened if Mary hadn't shown up.

The knife wielder cuts the three of us free, and I breathe a sigh of relief.

"How did you find us?" I ask Mary in a hushed voice. "We were . . . If you hadn't come, I don't know what would have happened to us."

She shrugs nonchalantly. "I told you I was going to distract the others for you. I did. And then I joined them when they came out looking for you. Very miffed about losing my intern, you know." She winks, and I crack a smile. "We were catching up to you. I wasn't sure what I was going to do when we did, but it turns out I didn't need to worry because you got yourselves caught by a village of bioluminescents. Colleen and the rest hightailed it back in the direction of the colony, and I followed after you."

"They are *not* going to make it back to the colony," Grayson says. "But I'm so glad you came down here."

"Oh, they'll make it back." Mary waves a hand.

I don't argue, but I'm with Grayson on this one. There's no way they survive the trip back. Some of the places we dropped down into, I can't imagine trying to get back up.

"Maybe they'll come to their senses and try for the exit instead," I say.

Mary laughs. "Sure."

One of the bioluminescents gestures for us to follow him, so we do. They're much more relaxed now, though it probably also helps that they took all our weapons when they captured us, and that Mary gave hers over voluntarily.

I'm still beyond terrified that they're going to slice us open. That if we make one wrong move, we'll be corpses.

Alice squeezes my hand, lets out a relieved breath. I really hope this is a good thing and not a leading-us-to-be-eaten thing. My gut tells me we're going to be okay, for now. My gut has been wrong a lot in the past, but I don't know. I think I'm getting better at reading it, understanding what it's actually telling me as opposed to what I think it's supposed to be saying.

We're led down a short tunnel, decorated with vines in swirly patterns down the walls, and emerge into another cavern, slightly larger than the first. It's filled with quite an array of things.

Skins in various stages of tanning. Meats being carved from the flesh of slain beasts and stored. People sewing and weaving and cleaning and hanging around. There's a steaming hot spring in one corner and it looks as though they are using this steam to cook things, which is brilliant, to be honest.

One of the bioluminescents who led us here rattles a chain of bones that hangs down from the ceiling near the tunnel opening. Everyone stops what they're doing and pays attention to him immediately. He's using their same language of gestures, but with bigger movements, like he's making sure everyone's able to see what he's saying. It occurs to me that communication must be really difficult for anyone here who can't see—especially since it doesn't appear these people have vocal cords at all, so I can't even think what they'd use as an alternative. I do notice that some of the farther-away people are gesturing among themselves.

By the time the man is done, *everyone* is gesturing among themselves. Grayson dips his head between mine and Alice's and whispers, "I think we might be hot gossip."

Alice covers her mouth with her hand to stifle a giggle. I am not so successful. The nearest bioluminescents look at me like I'm an alien, and I suppose I am.

A couple women come forward, and after a brief discussion with our guards, they take Mary, Alice, and me with them, leaving Grayson behind.

I don't like it.

But when I hesitate, Grayson nods.

So I go.

They keep our weapons but give us back the rest of our things. We're led through another short tunnel into a small alcove stuffed with several beds. The beds are made of woven plants and covered over with furs. They even have pillows, also made of furs.

Through their language—but with slower movements so that Mary and I can catch everything and relay it to Alice—our hosts explain that this is where we'll be sleeping. And then they start showing us different words in their language, based on our surroundings. I'm nervous about being separated from Grayson, though. It distracts me, and I have a hard time focusing. But I also want to be able to communicate well, so I try my best. Mary's lessons have been helpful, but I still know very little.

Mary, of course, is already pretty fluent, and I can tell they find her impressive. They take us on a cavern tour, pointing things out and showing us the gesture for them if we don't already know. I scrawl everything down in my notebook. Memorization is a particular strength for me. I should be able to go through this later and be passable.

"Does it worry you that they trusted us so fast?" Alice asks as we pass from the cavern where we were held hostage into a third large cavern. "I feel like . . . they could turn on us just as fast."

I frown. "I agree. But I think we're gonna have to go with it for now. Till they let us leave."

"*If* they let us leave," Alice adds.

I start to reply, but that's when we step into the third cavern. And it's *beautiful*, stunning beyond anything I've ever seen in my life or will ever see again even if I live to be one hundred. This cavern is smaller than the first two of the communal caverns, and I would bet anything its purpose is religious.

A waterfall spills down from the back of the room, dropping through an abyss in the floor to somewhere far below. Somewhere so far that the roar of the water is muted enough that I could hear someone speak in a whisper. Something luminescent must exist behind the waterfall, because it glitters, a riot of color.

The edges of the room are lined with enormous mushrooms, taller than me. They have that familiar mushroom shape, with bulbous stems topped by puffy half spheres. The undersides of the tops glow, sending light streaming down to the floor like spotlights. The rest of the floor is filled in with a chaotic assortment of plants and fungi, all bioluminescent, and all glowing the same shade of white blue. Thin stalactites—not bioluminescent—dangle from the ceiling at regular intervals, reaching almost to the floor. The only bare spot is a straight, narrow strip leading from the entrance to the waterfall. Or rather, to what looks like a shrine, built in front of the waterfall. The shrine is built of glowing stones, different from the ones we had in our village. The same stones encrust the ceiling of the cavern like a layer of coarse pink salt. Those making up the shrine have been cut and shaped into squares. The end result is a semicircle shape that radiates pink.

I feel this room inside my chest. The beauty of it punches me in the sternum. It feels like I've found my true religion, deep in the bowels of the earth, and it's whatever this room represents. Nature is just . . .

A tear drops onto my cheek, startling me. I brush it away and tell myself to pull it together because this is a ridiculous overreaction to the existence of a glowing room in a cave. I'm still trapped. Still a prisoner to these bioluminescent humans who don't speak our language and have clawed hands and sharp-toothed mouths.

After the shrine or the church or whatever they call the place, we go down another couple tunnels, some of which are lined with beds, some of which are too narrow for that and have beds situated in an alcove like the place I guess I can now refer to as "our room." We finally meet back up with Grayson in a storage alcove. It's cooler in this alcove—definitely not refrigerator cool, but chilly in my short-sleeved shirt—and they use it for keeping meat.

I resist the urge to run to Grayson, to cling and not let go.

"Are you all right?" Mary asks when we approach him, placing a gentle hand on Grayson's shoulder.

"I'm fine," Grayson answers. "They showed me . . . a bedroom, I guess?"

"Us too," says Alice.

"They seem to be trusting Mary, at least, right?" Grayson asks.

"I think so." It still discomforts me. *I* want to be the one they trust. I want to feel secure.

"Good. I think it's going to be okay here. I think we're going to be safe."

"Yeah."

I tell myself to relax. They've taken us in. They seem to be trusting us. And they haven't killed us.

Yet.

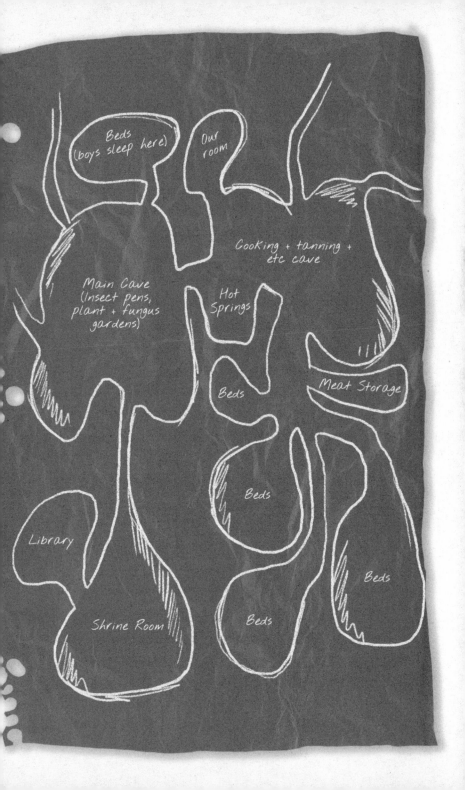

31

Good morning, Eliza. A bioluminescent girl joins me where I stand beside the fence surrounding one of the insect pens. She speaks to me in their language of gestures.

I reply the same way: *Good morning, Ama.*

It's been eight days since we arrived at the bioluminescents' village. It's almost as long as I spent in the colony. We've settled in here, and despite the language barrier, we've actually made friends.

Everyone's name has a gesture. Mary made up English-sounding names for us non-glowing humans to use, based on her best guess of the translation.

Did you want to help me feed the insects again today? Ama asks.

Yes, please.

These insects aren't like the ones we were eating back at the colony. They're mint green in color and have the shape of a stinkbug. The flat, shield-shaped bodies and long antennae. They're not bioluminescent, but the mint green is a bright enough color that I can forgive it. Fully grown, they're about two feet wide and three feet long, though their bodies sit pretty low to the ground. And they secrete a honeydew-like substance that the bioluminescents collect and use to sweeten recipes. When the insects get old—which is a matter of about a year— they're eaten. Seems like a pretty sweet way to live, if you ask me. Most insects don't get treatment like this, with food and mates brought to them. It reminds me of the farm that borders my parents' property. These insects are the underground version of livestock.

Ama passes me the basket of grass she was holding. Well, I'm calling it grass. I don't know what it is. It has a faint green luminescence to it, and it's about the consistency of grass, so. Close enough. I carefully open the gate to the pen and slip inside, transferring the grass to the insects' feeder. There are four creatures in each pen, and while they crowd me, excited for their breakfast, Ama checks for honeydew deposits. She gathers several, and then I help her clear out the small amount of insect manure that's accumulated since yesterday.

It's eerie, really, how similar the bioluminescents are to us. Our environments are so fully different, but the way we form communities and relationships, so similar.

After we're done feeding the insects, she takes me to the library.

They have a *library*.

They write on dried-out, broad-leaf plants with an inky substance harvested from insects. I can't begin to read their written language—scratches of lines and shapes and angles that mean nothing to me—but I love looking at it anyway.

Grayson, on the other hand, also loves the books. In fact, he's already in the library when we arrive. He's been determined to figure it out and does seem to be making some headway.

Ama's grimace-like expression at the sight of him makes me laugh. He asks a *lot* of questions about language.

"Eliza!" Grayson throws me one of his heart-melting grins. "I've gone full nerd and it's awesome."

"Uh, yeah." I sit beside him. "Looks like you have a new future career path as a linguist."

Grayson has been fully transformed by this village. He's smart, and I think he knew that somewhere deep down, but he's also strong and it seems like no one's ever told him he could be both. That he can be the guy who goes bow hunting and also the guy who sits on a porch with a good book. His incessant questions might drive Ama nuts, but the way he wants to fully immerse himself in learning has made him more attractive to me than ever.

I run my fingers over the brittle fibers of the paper in my hands. I wish I could take one, keep it as a souvenir.

So you've never met others like us before? I say to Ama.

I've never, she gestures, *but there is the legend of the plain-skinned man.*

"Grayson," I say aloud. He glances up. "Listen to this."

Ama straightens her spine. *The story is that he passed through here two generations ago. He had strange tools and wore strange body coverings—like you do—but he was friendly and he traded with our people and then he moved on. He was living with another village and he knew our language. Later, he returned, but only to scratch three lines into the wall. Then he disappeared forever.*

Grayson and I exchange a glance.

Can we see the marks? I ask.

Of course!

Ama leads us to a tunnel not too far from the library and there it is. Our familiar three lines.

"So we're still on our route," Grayson says to me.

"Yeah. And Mary's story about her grandfather . . . it has to be true."

I turn to Ama. *What's down this tunnel?*

She shrugs. *We don't go far down this one. Very dangerous creatures, plus another village who we have a bad relationship with.*

It's not what I want to hear.

But this conversation renews my faith in our plan.

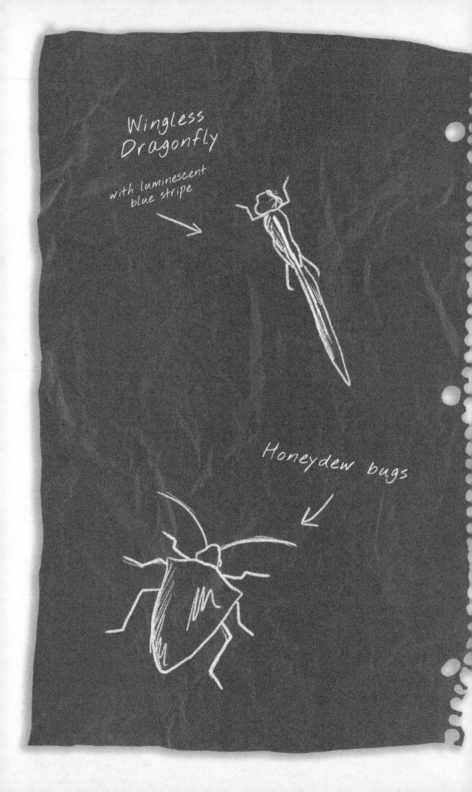

32

"Are we getting too comfortable here?" Grayson's voice startles me. I close my journal, where I was scribbling down notes about different types of glowite.

"I don't think so." But as I say it, I realize that I'm cozied up on my woven bed, knees up, back leaned against the wall while I write. The way I might sit on my bed at home—actual home.

This place feels so much more like an actual home than the colony. It's easy to forget that it's not where I'm meant to be.

"Maybe," I amend. I set down my journal and stand up.

Grayson looks worried and melancholy. I want to erase it, somehow. Wrap my arms around his waist and rest my head against his chest until he feels better. But I can't bring myself to do it.

Indecision tenses my shoulders. And, as usual, it's Grayson who moves closer to me. His hands slide down my sides, settle on my hips. "You still want to go home, don't you?"

"One hundred percent." My throat is sandpaper. "But I

think it's okay that we're resting a little bit here. I think it was needed, don't you? For morale."

"I guess. Yeah." His fingers tighten on my hips. "You promise, no plans to stay here?"

His eyes pierce mine, and I frown, edging back a step. "Can I ask you something?"

He nods, looking worried.

"I think . . . I noticed that a lot of the time, when you're closest to me, it's when we're talking about stuff like this. And then in between . . . I don't know what I'm asking. I want to go home no matter what we are. I'd want to go home even if you announced that you were staying right here. But I just . . ." I trail off. This is the worst speech ever.

Grayson doesn't move toward me again. He shoves his hands into his pockets. "So, I didn't hear a question in there." He pauses, smiling ever so slightly. "But what I took from your sentence fragments is that you don't know how interested I am in you."

I shrug and look away. My skin crawls with embarrassment.

"You do realize that I am a *much* more open book than you are?" His words startle me. "I think I've made it pretty clear how interested I am. *You,* on the other hand? I have no idea."

"I—oh." I chew a nail. "I'm sort of . . . You know I get anxious, talking to other people. Being around them. I'm always afraid I'm saying or doing the wrong thing. I'm constantly replaying conversations in my head and obsessing about whether something was dumb or insensitive or pointless or . . . you get the idea. I don't know how to . . . I like you so much, and it's scary. I don't know how to do it the right way."

"Is there a right or wrong way to have a relationship with someone when trapped in an underground cavern?"

I laugh. "I guess maybe there isn't a template, huh?"

"Not so much."

"Are you, um . . . saying we're having a relationship?"

He shrugs. "We seem to be?"

I take a step closer, bravely. Run both my hands up the back of his neck to clench in his hair. "We do have a pretty great 'how we met' story. Bet no one else's is similar."

"I sure hope not."

Our faces are so close, I can see every detail. Every long lash surrounding his beautiful green eyes. The stubble along his jaw, the two lone freckles on his nose. "Did you know," I whisper, trying to let myself be vulnerable, "that you might be the best person I've ever met?"

He cups my face in both hands. "Did you know that so are you?"

Our lips meet, gentle and teasing and soft. Like we have all the time in the world to do nothing but kiss. Which, really, we do. We're in a paradise. Grayson glides his hands slowly down my arms, his fingertips leaving goose bumps in their wake. I slip my hands beneath his shirt. Grayson is lean, courtesy of our not-quite-enough diet, but he's also muscular, courtesy of our physically demanding lives. Feeling ridged abs beneath my fingertips unknots something inside of me. I sort of can't believe that this beautiful human being is letting me touch him. That he's pressing his lips to the side of my throat and holding me close like this means just as much to him as it does to me.

It's not that I don't think I *deserve* what's happening right now. It's that I cannot believe I'm even capable of feeling such joy. Here. In this place. That I was lucky enough to find someone like Grayson, with his beautiful face and even better personality. And that he feels the same connection with me.

I didn't even know that I knew how to kiss like this until it happened. Kissing for me is usually as awkward and self-conscious as anything else I do. But when our mouths collide, everything else falls away.

I slide my fingertips down his cheeks, press the rest of myself closer. His hand rests on the small of my back, and the other twists in my hair as our kiss grows more heated. Kissing, suddenly, doesn't feel like enough, but I don't know where we go from here. He seems to feel the same, kissing me even harder and sliding his hand to the very bottom of my back.

A throat clears behind us. We break apart and I glance over Grayson's shoulder. It's Mary.

My cheeks flush with embarrassment. Luckily, the lighting isn't great in here, so it won't be noticeable.

"Sorry to interrupt," she says casually. "But I wanted to talk to the three of you."

That's when Alice peeks out from behind her shoulder, awkwardly.

"Sure! Of course." I sit on the bed, unsure what to do

with myself. Grayson sits, too, leaving a wide swath of space between us.

"I'm going to stay," Mary says unceremoniously. "Here in this village. I feel . . . at home here. I'm relatively safe and I can study this cavern, I can learn everything about it. This is my life's work; I feel so sure that it is."

"We don't belong down here, though," I say. "Even you."

Mary smiles sadly, leaning against the wall. "That's true, but it's also not true."

I furrow my brow. Alice folds her arms tight.

"How are we supposed to go the rest of the way without you?" Alice asks.

This time, Mary laughs. "You've been without me this entire time, and look how far you made it."

She's right; we did make it far. But we lost Eleanor. If Mary had been with us, maybe . . . I press my palms to my forehead, trying to squash the thought. Thinking about Eleanor shrivels me up inside. Her memory is a thousand knives shredding me to pieces.

"Hey." Mary places a tentative hand on my shoulder. "Please don't be upset. You know I have to stay."

I nod, but don't trust myself to speak anymore. Mary was never meant to come along with us. She fits in so well here. She truly does belong.

"One other thing I wanted to discuss," Mary goes on, "is what you plan to tell people when you leave."

"The . . . truth?" Grayson says.

"I . . . advise against that," says Mary. "I know times are different since my grandfather came down here, but it's almost worse if people believe you than if they don't."

"How?" Alice asks.

"The bioluminescents. This is their home. What if people are curious about this place, start drilling in? What happens to their homes, to *them*?"

I hadn't thought about this before. It unsettles me.

Alice starts to respond, but a long, loud wail cuts her off. Bioluminescents don't have vocal cords, so there's only one thing that could be making that noise: a tube of rock the bioluminescents use to create a warning noise during times of danger. It means everyone's supposed to take shelter in the shrine room.

I jump quickly to my feet, grabbing my backpack on instinct. Grayson's hand finds mine, and the four of us leave the alcove together. We melt into a crush of bodies outside our alcove, most pressing toward the shrine room, some standing their ground against the invaders, an army of what look like recently hatched, nearly knee-high spiders. They look similar to spiders I've seen before, so I know their venom isn't deadly, but there are *so many*. I freeze up at the sight of them. Luckily, Grayson keeps his wits and tugs me along.

We're blocked, though. The spiders dart wildly about, directly in our path to safety. We have only one escape that I can see, and it's the tunnel marked with three lines. The tunnel that leads away from our temporary sanctuary and back to our homes. Our *real* homes.

I squeeze Grayson's hand, and point. For all the utter chaos of the scene before us, everything is silent. A gentle clicking of jaws from the spiders, the padding of feet and the squelch of weapons rending arachnid flesh, and that's it. So I remain silent, too.

Grayson grabs Alice's arm, getting her and Mary's attention. He points, just like I did, and they both stare at the tunnel for what feels like much too long. Finally, Mary nods. She planned to stay, but she'll leave now, with us.

The four of us travel mostly in silence at first. It's quite an obstacle course down here now, cave formations everywhere, clotting up the tunnels. As we continue deeper, the tunnels continue to narrow, become more spiked with formations, more dangerous. None of us says anything, but we all know we're now outside the "safe zone" where the bioluminescents most commonly roam—although clearly, that wasn't so safe, either. We don't know what might be down here. How hungry it might be. How quickly we could be killed. They were so worried about us dying; it can't have been for no reason at all.

But we carry on, because we have to. We've reached the point of no return. The part of the video game where you can't go back and do side missions anymore, because you're too close to the end.

I weave through an obstacle course of thick stalagmites, all varying heights and shapes and girths. Alice is behind me, Grayson and Mary ahead.

There's a fatigue in my limbs that wasn't there when we set out the first time. It's not the fatigue of physical exertion, although that's there, too. It's just a bone-tiredness. I want this all to be over, I don't want to be fighting and clawing and struggling for my life.

It was easier not to think about it in the safety of the bioluminescent village, but there's a hole in my chest where Eleanor is missing. People say that sometimes, when a loved one dies, but I never got it. I see my chest as this place where my anxiety lives. It's where I get to feel all the pressing and twisting and aching and whirring. It's what works up my brain into cycling through all the social interactions I've ever had, and whether the person now hates me because of that dumb thing I said that one time seven years ago.

But now, I finally realize that there's more going on in my chest than anxiety. It's also the part that clutched tight to my friendship with Eleanor, and it's the part that most keenly feels her loss. Every time I think of her, a black hole opens up in my heart, and I'm just so incomplete.

Grayson catches his leg between two particularly close-together stalagmites. He pulls free, but the stalagmites have marked him with a scrape. He inspects it with a sigh that says, *This again*, and carries on.

If the wound were deeper, I'd make him stop so I could wrap it up, but this isn't worth the argument. We're *all* scraped up at this point.

We come to a halt at the center of a star-shaped collection of tunnels. Two of them angle down. And if there's a marking, we can't find it.

"I think we should split up," says Mary.

"That's a *terrible* idea," I disagree at once, my eyes scouring the walls for any signs.

"Not for long," she insists. "Just to see what these two tunnels here look like a little ways in."

"I sort of . . . think she's right," says Alice.

All the fight goes out of me. I can't anymore. "Okay."

"We all need to be very alert," says Mary, "so no offense to either of you, but, Grayson, you're going to come with me and, Eliza, you'll go with Alice."

I want to be offended, but who am I kidding? She's probably not wrong.

Alice and I start carefully down the left of the two chosen tunnels. I hold my glowite close to the walls, looking for any signs of markings or writing or just *something*. We're not supposed to go too far; Mary said to try to judge five minutes and then return. Like I have a clue what five minutes feels like anymore.

"I don't see anything at all helpful," Alice says in a dead voice.

"I know. Me neither."

"Can we just, like, sit for a minute or something?"

"Of course." I stop, crouch beside her worriedly. "You okay?"

She rests her face on her forearms. "Yeah. I just got a wave of exhaustion. Do you feel that way sometimes?"

"Pretty much all the time."

"I'm ready to be there. I'm sad and I'm tired and I just . . ."

"I know. I'm all of those things, too. But we're close; we have to be close. We can do this."

"We can." She sighs heavily. "Yes. We will make it. All of us. We *have* to."

But that's not how things go for us, of course. It's never how things go.

Because that exact moment is when we hear the horrible, wailing scream from somewhere not far ahead.

We look at each other for a fraction of a second, and then both break into a wild sprint.

Magma is the molten material known for shooting out the tops of volcanoes. It's made of molten rock, dissolved gas, and a bunch of other stuff. It's thousands of degrees warm. We get some really awesome rocks when it cools, above the earth's surface. We can only speculate about what it looks like when it's in the mantle.

I wonder what I'm going to feel like when I see it.

33

It's already too late when we arrive.

Blood is everywhere.

Dripping down the walls, puddling on the floor. It glows, extra sinister, in the light of the bioluminescent plants dangling from the ceiling. Which are also coated in the sticky crimson substance.

I see Grayson first, and I gasp. His face is splattered with gore, and he holds a stained knife in his fist. At his feet is something monstrous. It looks like an enormous crab, except it's covered in thick brown fur. My eyes sweep farther, and I fall to my knees.

Mary's head lies near the claw of the dead thing. Alice sees it, too, and she halts with a gasp. I glance behind us, to the tunnel we emerged from. My brain seems to be working more slowly right now; I can't piece this together. The tunnel that Grayson and Mary took exits right next to ours. So, if we hadn't decided to sit down, we might have been here for this, too.

I crouch, shaking, beside Mary's severed head. I don't even

know where her body is and I think I'm in shock. I think we're all in shock. Her eyes stare at me, wide and still glittering. The white inch of spine peeking out from her throat contrasts with the crimson that coats everything. Tubes of snapped veins and twists of sinew drape down to the floor.

I want to be sick but my organs won't do the work. I press fingertips to her smooth, pallid cheek. Mary. She seemed so invincible.

No one else has moved. I turn and rise slowly. Grayson has dropped his knife. I step cautiously around the mangled corpse of the crab creature, bending to retrieve the weapon. I hold it out to Grayson handle first.

"Are you okay?" I ask him.

"I'm fine." His voice is laced with pain. I sweep my eyes down the length of him until I find what's wrong. Deep teeth marks on an arm he's tried to angle away from me.

I don't say anything. Just turn and walk away, retrieving my backpack from Alice.

"What is that thing, and could there be more?" I ask, lifting Grayson's arm gently.

He watches me pour water over the serrated flesh. "Of course there are more. Someplace. Probably nearby. I think it's why the bioluminescents said it's too dangerous to come down here. It's very strong and very hard to kill."

I dab at the arm to absorb some of the excess water, but it's a lost cause anyway. The wound immediately wells up with blood. "How did you kill it?"

"Mouth," he answers, and winces. I'm wrapping gauze tight around his forearm.

"Okay." I step back. Press a hand to his blood-freckled cheek. "We know that now, I guess."

He nods. "I guess we do."

A droplet of blood lands on my hand. I grimace, look up.

And immediately wish I hadn't.

Mary's body dangles limply from a stalactite, impaled through her torso. The thing that beheaded her flung her body toward the ceiling and . . .

Mary didn't even want to come.

I squeeze my eyes shut. "We need to get out of here," I say in my very calmest voice.

Grayson nods. He peels himself away from the wall, eyes darting upward edgily. His fist tightens on the hilt of the knife, and then he's following me. I hope Alice is, too. I am trying to be brave and strong and get us away from here, but all my energy is going into maintaining the numbness I feel right now. Not letting myself think about Mary or the fact that we're down to three again or the full horror of the carnage I just walked into.

Keep going down. Mary's words echo in my head. *Down, down, down until you hit magma. Until it's so hot you think you'll melt. Then start looking for the way up.*

For the time being, that's all we can do.

Every step feels heavier than the last. Every time we come to an intersection of tunnels, or emerge into a bigger cavern, I flinch away from it, sure we'll come across hungry wildlife. We don't, though, at least not for the time being.

When we reach a stream, all of us stop to clean up a bit and refill our water bottles.

"Eliza," Grayson says, his voice dead. "Do you think it's okay that we left Mary . . . where she was?"

"I think . . . we had to." I swallow hard, not wanting to think about it. About the fact that we left Eleanor to be devoured by bloodthirsty grubs, and left Mary in pieces. We did these things because we had to if we wanted to survive. But our insides are slowly and steadily becoming more dead.

"You're right." Grayson's voice gets hoarse. He glances down at his arm, bleeding through the gauze. "I just . . ."

A silence yawns between us.

"Let me change the gauze," I say. "You should wash that, while we're here."

He listens to me, like I know what I'm talking about. Winces while he unwraps the gauze, dips his arm into the water to wash the wound clear. The flesh around it is red and puffy. Not great.

"I know," he says tonelessly when I carefully start to wrap it. "It doesn't look good."

"It, um . . ." I wrap faster so I don't have to look at it anymore. "The magma can't be far, and then we'll get you the medical care you need."

"Sure."

We're battered and bloodstained, all three of us. I'm saying the words as though I believe them, but Grayson can't even muster that. He's not as lucky as me, though. I only witnessed the aftermath. I didn't have to see that thing fling Mary's body to the ceiling, didn't have its razor teeth chew open my arm.

I glance at Alice. She's swirling her fingers in the water, a bit upstream, looking lost and alone. She had *just* said we needed to all make it out of here, and now Mary's gone. I want to say something to make her feel better, but when I think about what I'd want someone to say to *me* about Eleanor or Mary, I can't come up with a single thing. None of it would fix anything. None of it would repair the ever-widening hole in my chest. The numbness overtaking me, crawling through my veins like a virus.

"Let's go," I say, loudly enough for both of them to hear. Because we're doing nothing, and it seems like they're waiting for instruction.

Not from me, it can't be from me.

But apparently they'll take instruction from anyone now, because they listen, following me to the end of the cavern, where our only exit is via a short waterfall down into another glittering cavern.

As we continue on our way, I have all these worries at the back of my mind, except they don't even feel like worries. They don't feel like anything. They just exist.

I've barely even thought about the colony since we reached the bioluminescent village. What would Colleen say now? She'd be so smug. Five of us abandoned her, three of us remain, and one of us has an infected wound that will surely kill him if we don't make it back to the surface soon. We've really messed up, haven't we?

There's nothing to do about that now. Nothing to do except keep walking, like half-dead zombies, going through the motions.

If anything attacks us, I don't even know that I have the strength to fight it off.

Kill it with a knife down its throat.
Give the blade an extra twist.
For revenge.

34

As we continue deeper, I feel more and more numb. I don't even feel anxious anymore. I'm so worn down that even my most predictable trait has gone dormant. Nothing has made me anxious in the hours since Mary's death. Not even the tunnels we passed that definitely had creatures in them. Or the things that came out to greet us. The things we had to kill.

My clothes are saturated now, with blood and ichor. Stains that will never come out, that stiffen the fabric and make it scratch against my skin with every step I take. I wonder if this is what people feel like who live in war zones. If this is what I would feel like were an apocalypse to come. The complete all-consuming nothingness is welcome and it's awful, all at once.

We reach another star-shaped intersection, and it gives me a tiny thrill of anxiety. Oh no. But also: finally. The numbness was unnatural. It couldn't last.

Grayson and Alice stand in the middle, hesitant. I start to feel panicked. There's no way this is the case, but . . . what if it's the *same* star-shaped intersection? What if, somehow, we've circled back around? What if we die here, slowly, in the tunnels. Or quickly, murdered by avenging bioluminescents or monster crabs.

"Which one do you think, Eliza?" Alice asks me.

"I, um . . . the . . . give me a second, I have to think about it."

"Of course!" Alice physically steps back from me, like her nearness is the reason I haven't figured it out yet.

Two of the tunnels are basically identical. A third and fourth also slope down, but not as much. I should rule them out, based on the "whichever one goes down steepest" criteria, but something in my gut won't let me. I pace back and forth in front of all the tunnels, frozen with indecision. Why aren't their markings here, either? It seems like the place to have markings is the intersection with eight choices, more important than the intersection with two.

"Eliza?" Alice moves hesitantly to my elbow. "Do you want to talk it through with us?"

I stare at her. Then at Grayson with his sheen of infection sweat and his labored breathing.

And I melt down.

Hard.

"I can't do this." I slump down, the ridges of the wall scraping my back. "I'm not a leader, you guys. This is when we need Mary the most. She knew everything, *understood* everything. I don't know what I'm *doing*. You're trusting me and why would you *ever* trust me? I'm just a girl who loves rocks and would do anything her best friends said to just so they wouldn't think she was a boring old pile of nothing." I start to cry. I can't control myself. The cap has come off the soda bottle, and I'm frothing everywhere. "But I *am* a pile of nothing. I didn't *want* to come to the swamp. I didn't want to go to any of the parties or try the beer or climb the fence to the football field and streak across it in my bra. But I didn't want to be alone and I didn't want to be not good enough and look at my punishment. Everyone's dying around me, I'm just *toxic*. I'm—"

"Eliza, *stop*." Alice grabs me by both shoulders, and it startles me enough that I do stop, for a moment. "I know you're upset, but you have to pull it together. Because you know what? Maybe you weren't a leader when you came here, but you're a leader now. Leaders aren't the people who know the most or are the best qualified or have perfect confidence full-time. They're the people who *lead*, and I gotta tell you, you've been doing it. You're quiet and you're gentle but you know what you want even if you don't think that you do. Your friends are jerks, I've already told you that. They're terrible. But you know what? I'm grateful to them. Because they got you here, and that means I have a prayer of going home, finally. *Finally*. None of us got the courage to do this till you came, remember? You did this. You led us out."

The tears won't stop flowing down my cheeks. I drop my face onto my knees, trembling and sobbing. "But we might not make it. What if I let you down, like I already let down Mary and Eleanor?"

"Hey, you did *not* let them down," says Grayson, crouching

beside me. He lays his good arm across my hunched shoulders. "Don't let yourself think like this, Eliza; it's not a healthy path. We need you. It's like Alice said. None of us were ready to go till you came. You don't need to be anybody else. You don't need to be braver or stronger or fun in the exact right way. You don't need to be anything except the Eliza we know. *That's* the Eliza we love."

"I am being so pathetic," I murmur into my knees.

"No, you're not." Alice squeezes my hands. "You're not being pathetic at all. There's nothing wrong with sharing your feelings. I do it all the time! It feels good. Let it all out. Every last bit, so we can get ourselves on home."

I am ready to be home. I am *so* ready. My mind fills with visions of my parents and my sisters. My house, my *room*. I even miss my school. The routine of the school day was everything to me.

Meg and Sherri were not my only friends. The revelation comes to me with an abrupt burst of clarity. Neither one of them was even in most of my classes, once I started taking AP and focusing on the sciences. I could name, right now, at least seven people who I can't wait to see. Who I would consider calling and inviting over to hang out. Why didn't I ever do it? Why did I refuse to let myself see that there were plenty of people who liked talking to me? Who didn't tell me I was an insufferable nerd and didn't make me feel like they wished I'd just shut up every time I opened my mouth.

Those were my real friends. Those, and these two people standing before me right now.

And right now, *these* friends need me. They need me more than Meg and Sherri ever have. I learned a lot from those friendships, things I didn't realize. I can take the good pieces, I can take the hurt and the pain, and I can turn it into something good. I will not let Alice and Grayson down.

Slowly, confidently, I get to my feet. I hug them each in turn, even though I think it scares them, and then I turn back to the tunnels, facing them with hands on my hips.

"That one." I point confidently at a tunnel angled slightly to the left. "I know it isn't the steepest decline, but it actually has a little bit of a breeze, and a noticeable temperature increase. I think we're close."

I turn around and smile, broadly. "I think we're really close."

35

I love being right.

I have never loved being right so much as I love it at this particular moment.

After countless hours of traversing an increasingly steep and treacherous tunnel, we've done it: We've found the earth's mantle.

How we are not dead, burnt to a crisp, is beyond me, because the room we find ourselves in is what can only be described as a magma chamber. The air is dry as a fireplace. It pulls heavy and searing hot through my lungs. We're surrounded by obsidian. The walls, floors, everything here is made of it. Including all the incredible and unique rock formations throughout the room. I walk through it like a museum, not touching anything, just observing.

There's very little bioluminescence here. A cluster of mushrooms in one corner, but that's it. Everything else is just blackness.

Well. *Almost* everything else. Because there's a bright glow of orange emanating from another corner. It's *magma*. Real, honest-to-God, not-from-a-volcano magma. I can't get too close to it because it sends fry-the-skin-off-your-face waves of heat that knock me back, but it pulls an emotional response I would never have expected out of my chest. I'm sobbing with the sheer beauty of it. Of actually making it to the bottom of the earth's crust, to see evidence of the mantle with my own eyes.

"Eliza? You okay?" Grayson crouches beside me.

I nod, wiping away my tears. "It's just—no one is meant to be able to *see* this. Not with our current technology, not standing ten feet away from it. It's so—it's *magical*. I know that's a ridiculously nerdy thing to say, but it's true."

Grayson slips an arm around my back. "Listen, I don't know a thing about geology besides what you and Mary have taught me. But even I know this is a big deal."

My throat swells, I fight back another wave of tears. "I wish she were here to see it. I don't even think—she never really wanted to leave this place, I don't think. But I know she would have wanted to see *this*." I swallow hard. "But she was right. We made it. And look—do you see that tube over there, leading up? I'd bet anything it takes us back to the surface."

Grayson swipes a finger discreetly beneath his eye. I don't say anything about the fact that he's crying because I know he doesn't want me to, but I don't blame him.

"Is this it?" Alice asks, approaching. "Is this what we wanted?"

"Yeah." My voice comes out hoarse. "Yeah, it is. You guys, we made it."

We didn't *all-the-way* make it, not yet. But upon further inspection of the structure I'm calling a lava tube, even though that isn't quite what it is, I feel more confident than ever. For the first time since I fell through that sinkhole, I have true hope. Not the half-hearted hope I clung to before, where I kept telling myself there had to be a way, and went through all the motions, determined and bullheaded. Now the hope is so thick and so real, it sits in the cavities in my heart left by Eleanor and Mary, and it plugs them up. It's not a solid fill; it's like reattaching a car bumper with duct tape. But it gets the job done as well as I need it to for now.

We've decided to stay here for the night—or for what we *think* is the night, because with our traveling, we have less concept of time than ever. But we want to be well rested when we depart. So we set up a little camp in the middle of the cavern, eat most of the food we have remaining, and reminisce.

"What are you going to do first when you get home?" Alice asks.

"Eat something that's not made of insect or fungi," Grayson answers immediately. We all laugh, and agree.

"I'm really excited to sleep in my bed with my warm, dry sheets and my nice soft mattress," I add.

"Take a shower with soap," says Grayson. "And, you know, go to the hospital."

I frown. He's been handling his wound pretty stoically, but it's starting to really fester. It stinks when I remove the gauze, and the angry red has worsened into a purplish sheen, oozing yellow pus.

"The hospital will be our first stop," I say, resting a hand on his knee.

"And we'll bring you fast food or something," Alice adds, "because hospital food is *not* what you want for your first meal back on the earth's surface."

"Oh please." I scoff. "Like they're going to let any one of us out once the three of us walk into a hospital."

"Good point." Alice smiles. "But I guarantee I could get my parents to bring us any food we wanted."

"Mine, too," I add.

"My mom makes the *best* steak," says Grayson with a wistful sigh.

Talk of food and friends and family keeps us going for quite a while, but eventually we get tired and decide to sleep.

While the others settle in, I clean out my backpack of excess glowite and other supplies we won't need anymore, wanting it to be as light as possible before our ascent in the morning. At the bottom, I find something I can't believe I'm just seeing for the first time.

"Glenn left us a note in here," I say.

"Really? What's it say?" Alice perks up.

I sit cross-legged between them. "It says, 'You deserved to be free.' And he signed it."

"Wow." Alice blinks against tears. "I hope he's doing fine back there. I hope they all are."

I lie down, exhausted now. We thought Glenn was the dangerous one, when all along, it was Colleen. "I hope so, too."

We settle in for the night, bone-tired and eager to get home. None of us keeps watch, even, because there's no point. It's extremely hot in here. Bearable, but unpleasant. Between that and the magma, we're confident nothing will come looking for us here.

"Are you feeling okay?" I ask Grayson, though he is clearly *not* feeling okay.

"I'm fine." He pulls me to his side. "I have to be fine."

"But—"

"Eliza," he sighs. "We're going to make it out of here tomorrow. I can last until then. I promise."

I nestle closer to his side, rest a hand on his stomach. His skin is too warm, even for our current atmosphere, but I try not to let it worry me. There's nothing I can do, so I have to believe him when he says that he's fine.

"You have to make it out of here with me," I whisper. "I've gotten kind of attached to you."

He lets out a soft huff of laughter. "I've gotten kind of attached to you, too."

I press a soft kiss to his cheek and then use his shoulder as a pillow, closing my eyes, content. Old Eliza would have thought this was beyond scandalous, sleeping curled up with a boy. New Eliza knows that as intimate as it is, it's not intimate like *that*. It's just comforting, listening to the low hum of his sleeping breath.

Our last night here, I think, with that same sense of hope and optimism pounding in my chest.

And then I will be home.

We're. Going. Home.

36

Our morning is leisurely. It's almost like now that the time has come to depart, we're not sure how to go about it.

The lava tube has a smooth texture, ringed like an esophagus, and with a sharp incline. None of us is super confident about how it'll go when we start to climb, and we don't know how long it'll take. Nerves buzz in my stomach. All three of us are quiet as we gather our things and prepare to depart.

"This is going to be tough," I say. "We're not really going to be able to rest, and I know we're all so tired already."

Grayson's face is grim and pale. Looking at him turns my gut into claws, but I don't want him to know how worried I am about his health.

"Are we ready?" I ask, because neither of them has spoken.

"I'm ready," says Alice, determined.

Grayson ducks his head up into the tunnel. "It's hot in there," he says.

"Yeah." I shake my full water bottle in his direction. "We're going to have to ration this."

"I don't . . . I mean, I guess I'm ready."

I slip my arms around his waist, rise to my toes, and kiss his cheek. His too-warm cheek.

"I know you're not feeling well," I tell him. "But we're so close."

He smiles down at me. "I think the hard part is only beginning."

I sigh. "Such a negative attitude."

"We can do it," Alice says confidently. "We're strong. We've been through so much. It's time."

We are traveling up the tube for what feels like forever. We can't stop and rest because there's nowhere *to* stop. The only thing that keeps us going is our complete and utter desperation to reach home.

The spot where we reached the earth's mantle is likely close to twenty miles from the surface. Now we're going pretty close to straight up. If we were walking at a fast pace, we could do it in eight or nine hours, but we're not walking, and our pace is not brisk. It's probably going to be double that, if not more. It's killing us.

My arms ache, my legs have turned to blobs of mush. I don't know how long I can go on like this. How long any of us can go on. Especially Grayson. He made me overtake him, because he's breathing too hard, falling behind, and he doesn't want to knock me loose with him if he slips. I keep glancing down. The gap between us keeps increasing, even as I continue to widen the gap between Alice and me so as not to leave him behind.

And then he stops. He lays his whole body on the sloped part of the tube like he's completely given up. I scramble down to him without a thought.

"Grayson, you have to get up," I say, running my fingertips through his hair. He's pouring with sweat. We all are; it's a billion degrees in here, though it has cooled as we have moved upward. But Grayson is the worst. He looks sickly, his skin unnatural in hue.

"I can't," he murmurs. "I'm not gonna make it, Eliza. Please—go with Alice. Leave me here."

"I can't do that." My eyes fill with tears. "I'm not leaving you here."

"I'm dying." He lifts his head. "I'm dying and I have no strength left." He reaches for my hand, holding it in his, which burns with fever. "I love you and I want you to go. Please."

I cannot think of what to say. It makes me angry. "That's not fair at all, Grayson. You don't get to tell me that you love me and then in the next breath tell me I'm supposed to abandon you. I'm not an abandoner. That is one thing I don't do, will *never* do. I love you, too, you know."

"You can't just sit here with me," he says angrily. "You can't *stay*, Eliza; you have to get out."

"I'm not letting you go, not when we're so close to the end. We have to make it, Grayson. You are *going* to make it."

"I'm not," he insists. And then we're at a stalemate. I'm not leaving but he's not moving and I don't know what we can do about it.

Until Alice arrives. "Hey, what's the holdup?" she says impatiently. "I got to the top! But then I saw you guys weren't even with me."

My head snaps up. "Seriously?"

"Yeah! Let's go."

"I can't," Grayson says, his voice faint.

Alice narrows her eyes, glances between the two of us. "All right. You listen to me and you listen *close*. We have already lost two people. We're not losing any more. *I'm* not losing any more. We have come *too far* for this defeatist attitude." She turns to me. "Feeling strong?"

"Extremely."

"Me too. Let's haul him up."

We emerge into a tiny alcove, fronted by deep water. All that's between us and the surface world is a short swim under a stone overhang.

I make Grayson go first, then drop into the water after him. The cave is shallow, and I can actually see the sun shining into the entrance. It hurts my eyes. We did it. *We made it.*

Grayson is clinging to a rock on the other side, eyes squinting. He grabs my hand as I swim through.

"Oh my God, the sun," Alice says when she emerges. She climbs up the rocky shore and slips her hands through her hair, squeezing out the water. "Let's go!"

"Wait!" I stumble up behind her and grab her shirtsleeve. "Before we go, I was thinking . . . we need to decide what we're going to say about . . . where we were."

"Obviously, we're just going to tell people what happened," says Alice, confused.

"But what if that means people get sent down to explore? What does that do for the bioluminescents?" I swipe back my dripping hair. "I think we should say we just survived with each other. That we found each other and then kept walking until we got here. I just . . . It doesn't seem like our place to disturb the bioluminescents' lives like that. We don't know what'll happen if other humans go down there looking for them, but we know it won't be good. We haven't even figured out how to treat people of our same species as equals yet; I can only imagine what we'd do with them."

Alice frowns. "I guess that's a good point. But what about the colony?"

"Well," says Grayson. "I think we all made choices. They made the choice to stay; we made the choice to leave. The bioluminescents didn't make any choices at all; they just live where they've always lived, until we interrupted. I think Eliza's right about this."

"All right," I say. "Then we're agreed."

I reach into my soggy backpack and pull out my journal. It got damp during this very last part of our journey, and the ink bleeds, but it's still legible. I flip through a few pages, kiss its cover, and then tear out the innards and scatter them across the surface of the cave pond. A moment of regret flits through me, only because of all the scientific discoveries and memories scribbled within those pages. But this was the right thing to do.

"Goodbye, old Eliza," I whisper as the pages absorb water, as the ink smears further. I am not the same girl who started keeping this journal. I will never be her again.

And as the three of us step out into the sunlight, hand in hand, I'm okay with that.

ACKNOWLEDGMENTS

I am eternally grateful to:

Sarah LaPolla, my tireless agent.

Amanda Maciel, my brilliant editor.

Everyone at Scholastic who worked on this book and helped make it the polished, beautiful product you see before you.

My endlessly supportive family.

And my friends. Friendships—good and bad—are such a huge theme in this book, and I'm lucky to have some truly great friends in my life. From the hags to the hen house, I have definitely found my people.

Cara and I are on our way to the commune. The Haven. As we predicted, our boyfriends wanted to come, too, and Gavin volunteered to drive us in his truck. Given the quality of the roads we have to take to get there, that's both a great and a horrible thing. It'll be harder for this truck to get stuck in a muddy rut, but it's also been a bit of a rough ride. And part of me absolutely can't believe we're doing this.

Cara called the Firehorse guy who runs this place. I listened on speakerphone while she talked to him. It was all a load of major hippie crap. He actually said stuff like, "I would delight in welcoming you to our serene little corner of nature." Let me tell you, serene is not how I feel when I'm in nature, but Cara was way into the whole thing, and it's pretty much all she's been excited about yet this summer, so here we are.

And Firehorse wasn't lying. We are thoroughly ensconced in nature. What started out as a paved road has turned into two rutted, barely visible tracks as we've gone deeper into the wild. The closer the tree branches get to the sides of Gavin's truck, the more apprehensive I become. But I'm excited, too. I've never been to one of these off-the-grid places before, and I've always been curious. There's something comforting about the whole concept. Constructing a civilization for yourself outside of society where you all harmoniously coexist and don't have to worry about stressful stuff like money and college and careers.

"Did you know this place was so far out here?" Jackson asks Cara. And he does not use a nice tone.

"It's not *that* far," Cara replies. She's pretending to inspect the ends of her honey-blonde hair, but she catches my gaze in the rearview mirror and in that fraction of a second, we have a transmission that doesn't require words or even a change in expression. The message is: *No, neither of us had any idea we were going this far into nowhere.*